ONE MORE RIVER

ONE MORE RIVER

Suzanne Pierson Ellison

Serenade/Serenata
BOOKS
of the Zondervan Publishing House
Grand Rapids, Michigan

A Note From The Author
I love to hear from my readers! You may correspond with me by
writing:

> Suzanne Pierson Ellison
> 1415 Lake Drive, S.E.
> Grand Rapids, MI 49506

ONE MORE RIVER
Copyright © 1985 by The Zondervan Corporation
Grand Rapids, Michigan

Serenade/Serenata is an imprint of Zondervan Publishing House,
1415 Lake Drive, S.E., Grand Rapids, Michigan 49506.

ISBN 0-310-47022-6

All Scripture quotations, unless otherwise noted, are taken from the
HOLY BIBLE: NEW INTERNATIONAL VERSION (North
American Edition). Copyright © 1973, 1978, 1984, by the Interna-
tional Bible Society. Used by permission of Zondervan Bible
Publishers.

Edited by Pamela M. Jewell
Designed by Kim Koning

Printed in the United States of America

85 86 87 88 89 90 91 / 10 9 8 7 6 5 4 3 2 1

To my mother
who taught me how to translate
1 Corinthians 13 into everyday life

CHAPTER 1

SWEET AND CLEAR with the magic that only a gifted singer can project, Amy Shelby's voice drew music out of the disparate young voices that rose eagerly from the confines of the middle-aged Maverick that lumped along the twisting mountain road. The trio of youngsters had all but exhausted her extensive repertoire of "getting in the mood for summer church camp" songs, but she had managed to keep them busy and out of trouble on the long, dusty ride to Camp Colina. In a sense she welcomed their noisy exuberance; it prevented her from dwelling on her own dark thoughts. But now that the trip was almost over, she released them to their rising excitement and tried to concentrate on the dwindling dirt trail which, if memory served, would eventually lead them to their destination.

Amy was certain that the northern California side of the Sierra Madre range held the original patent on the scent of pine; the air literally tingled with the crisp fresh breath of a mountain forest in early summer. It was still hot and clear at five o'clock, but she knew that when the sun disappeared in a few hours a chilly mist would take over the valley that cradled the camp in its arms. Of course the blazing fire behind the rough log altar during the nightly vesper service had always been enough to warm the mellow campers after a busy day on the trails. But Amy would not be there when the fire was lit tonight—not for the warmth, not for the group communion with God.

She shouldn't have been anywhere near Camp Colina on this lovely afternoon in June. The camp was on her list of things to avoid these days . . . things that still goaded her to self-directed anger and tugged at her pain after all this time. She had tried to tell herself that this was just a scenic drive, after all, a family obligation. She would deliver the kids and turn around without a second glance at the scene of her deepest childhood religious discoveries . . . the source of a lifetime of loving family memories.

But when she saw the familiar old sign, handpainted on a massive piece of redwood bark, she knew there was no escaping the omnipresent intimacy of Camp Colina. No escaping the haunting memory of the last time she'd seen her mother . . . no escaping the unextinguished pain of her mother's subsequent death.

Why did Dad volunteer me for this trip? she asked herself, suddenly angry with the one parent she still had near her. *Why did Kay have to come down with the flu? Why did she agree to be a camp counselor this week anyway? And why on earth had Dad married her so soon after Mother's death?*

Of course, from her father's point of view six or seven years was hardly a brief period of mourning. But then again he'd only had to cope with the loss; his pain was free of guilt. His memories of Amy's mother were unstained by adolescent selfishness . . . careless teenage choices that had resulted in tragedy. In time he had retired her cherished image to his photo album

8

and reached out for another loving woman and her chestnut-haired, perpetual motion child. He had learned that Kay's earlier widowhood had given her the special grace to understand her new husband's grief. But Amy had already left the nest by then, busy with her life as a high school band leader and private music teacher. Although she lived less than half an hour from her childhood home near San Francisco, she generally avoided that tomb of her mother's memory—where Kay Shelby now reigned in her mother's kitchen and slept in her mother's bed.

Kay was so kind to her husband's daughter, so patient and loving and unimposing, that Amy could not begin to justify the resentment she still felt toward her. But resent her she did, just as she resented this bouncing, bubbling small boy beside her . . . a child with nothing but goodness and hope in his heart. Even though she'd been drafted to deliver Joey and his two look alike redheaded friends to camp, Amy was secretly glad that she'd had a chance to do something kind for him. They truly had enjoyed the ride up together.

"We're here!" Joey shrieked, delighted by the circle of pines that served as a parking lot. "This is it, huh, Amy? The place you always went with your other mother?"

Trying to suppress the anguish that his eager, thoughtless words triggered within her, Amy parked the car and answered softly, "This is Camp Colina."

The tiniest wisp of a breeze served to welcome the children as they bounded out of the car, leaping like pronghorn deer at dusk after a sweltering summer day.

Amy followed with considerably less exuberance. Slowly her eyes took in the fragrant, spring green meadow and the circled wagon train of half-open cabins that surrounded it. Grizzly, Timber Wolf, Cottontail, Raccoon. Every name lived in some sweet

9

corner of the Camp Colina closet of her mind. Old feelings of love and peace wrestled with newer ones of pain and loss, blocking the air from her throat.

Fighting the memories that assailed her, she turned her attention to the handcut redwood tables and benches that flanked the main lodge. At the moment the whole area was inundated with giggling clusters of tiny children and mismatched heaps of luggage, sleeping bags, and teddy bears. Here and there a grownup smiled or laughed or tossed a welcoming arm around a young newcomer.

Supervising the genial commotion was a tall blond man with a battered clipboard and an utterly irresistible smile. In dusty blue jeans and a forest green Camp Colina tee-shirt, his apparel hardly distinguished him from his peers. But something in his bearing did. Amy could not place what it was, exactly. He was at least thirty, but his build was light, his motion energetic. He had short sandy hair and sea blue eyes and a face that was nice but not unforgettable. Yet he carried himself with the aura of one who is satisfied with his place in the universe, not smug but richly content in the knowledge that he is in exactly the right place at the right time doing precisely the job he was preordained to do. How Amy envied him!

A dark-haired woman in her forties came up to ask the man a question. He put his arm around her as though he'd known her all his life, his eyes shining with laughter at some indecipherable joke she must have made. With a cheerful laugh of her own, she grabbed one of the little girls by the hand and headed up toward the northside cabins.

Little redheaded Cindy watched with interest, leaning a bit closer to Amy. "I hope she's *my* counselor," she murmured wistfully, recalling Amy to her purpose here. She had come to Camp Colina to deliver her "Three Musketeers," not to recarve ancient wounds.

10

"I hope so, too," she answered, not entirely by rote. If all the counselors up here were like the brunette, Amy's tiny charges were in good hands. "Let's go ask—"

Her voice stopped as she spied Joey hurtling himself toward the man with the clipboard. She was quickly learning that her little "brother" always operated at full-speed, rarely giving any thought to his actions unless some unfortunate consequence forced him to.

As the boy reached the man, clinging to his leg like a boisterous puppy, Amy felt a surge of anxiety. Joey was so terribly immature! Even with his mother here it might have been a mistake to let him come so soon. Without her he would be lost, homesick and frightened. And worse yet, he could be rejected by the more mature children, who might find his boundless enthusiasm too reminiscent of a stage they'd barely outgrown.

None of these concerns were mirrored on the tall man's face as he crouched down to meet Joey on his own level. Instead of tousling his hair like so many might have done, he reached out and shook the little boy's hand, man to man. Joey seemed to flower, mature just a tiny bit before Amy's eyes. He continued addressing the man eagerly, pointing toward his stepsister and his two friends. Slowly straightening, the man checked his clipboard for a few seconds and then headed toward Amy, a smile of welcome on his face.

She knew it was his standard greeting-the-campers smile, but that didn't make it any less appealing. Wide dimples graced his full lips, adorning a grin that was half boy-next-door, half virile man in his prime. Amy wasn't sure which part she responded to, but her answering smile was spontaneous and unchecked.

"I'm Adam Reed," he greeted her, holding out his hand. "I'm in charge of this circus. And you're—"

11

"Amy Shelby!" Joey declared with equal parts pride and volume. "My big sister!"

Amy was a bit surprised by Joey's enthusiastic if not wholly accurate declaration, but she gave him an indulgent grin before she slipped her hand into Adam's. To her surprise, his skin was warm and soothing . . . yet not so soothing, really, in an inexplicable but utterly delightful way.

Abruptly she found herself wishing that she'd bothered with make up this morning. Her plain red tee-shirt, adorned with a musical staff and the first four notes of Beethoven's Fifth Symphony, seemed dull and uninspired. Her cutoff jeans had been great in the heat, but somehow failed to convey the moment of elegance she suddenly longed for.

But Adam Reed didn't seem to notice her clothes. His eyes swept over her flowing black hair and enormous gray eyes, richly lashed even without mascara, and for a moment he seemed to crawl right into her soul. Without conscious knowledge Amy's hand closed around his, and her eyes met his with mute but perfect communion.

In less than a moment he looked away, causing Amy to think she'd imagined that searing moment. Belatedly he released her hand to greet the other two children. The warmth of his palm lingered on hers.

"You must be Cindy and Nathan," he sagely deduced.

Cindy giggled and Nathan grinned. They were always pleased when someone called them each by name instead of making ubiquitous reference to "the twins."

"How did you guess?" Joey asked, clearly awed at Adam's perception.

Again he checked his clipboard, even though Amy was sure he had already memorized the cabin assignment for each of his tiny charges. "Nathan, you're going to be staying in Raccoon Cabin with a great ball player, Mark 'Grand Slam' Ferris. Cindy's going to be in Chipmunk, and Joey here will be in Grizzly."

"I'm a grizzly bear! I'm a grizzly bear!" Joey hollered, punctuating his remarks with growling bruin sounds. "Can we get our stuff now?"

When Amy nodded, the three children took off for the car, each seizing whatever he or she valued most. Adam turned back to Amy, his golden smile still in place. She wasn't sure if it always lived on his face or was visiting there just for her, so she tried to restrain the sunbeams that threatened to paint her own delighted visage.

"Kay was assigned next door to Joey, in Timber Wolf," he began in a rich, soothing baritone that could have held her attention for a month. "I guess you know we have cabin families here—a boys' cabin with a girls' cabin." Then he broke the spell by adding, "Your mother said you'd been here many times before."

"Kay is not my mother," Amy replied without thinking, her voice surprisingly harsh. It wasn't at all what she meant to say to this exciting man, and certainly not the tone his presence engendered in her heart! As she struggled for words to take back her faux pas, Adam's startled eyes swept back over her, shielding just a hint of concern.

"I'm sorry," he told her as if he really meant it. "I'm new to this part of the world myself, and all I know about these people is what I've heard from their pastors."

Amy looked away. "Please forgive me, Adam. I didn't mean to snap at you. I just. . . ." She stopped, knowing she couldn't explain her inner turmoil to a stranger, even one as open and friendly as this one. *Especially* one as open and friendly as this one. She had trouble even remembering basic English when he touched her with that smile! "Kay married my father six months ago," she forced out. "She plays the organ at their church."

13

Amy didn't realize at first that she'd said *their* church, not *my* church or even *our* church, although she'd been baptized there and Kay had only been a member for two years! But when was the last time she'd gone to a service—any service, at any church? What right had she to claim anything that had to do with Christ?

Trying to pick up the conversation without upsetting her again, Adam offered, "I know she's a musician. That's one of the reasons I was excited about having her up here this week. When she called me this morning she said that you were even more gifted in that department."

Amy shrugged. It was nice that Kay had given her a compliment, but it wasn't necessarily true. Her musical skills were more diverse than Kay's—she played a dozen instruments well enough to teach them and had a beautiful singing voice. But Kay really had more keyboard talent . . . perhaps because she had given herself to that one thing whereas Amy had retreated from the piano the instant her mother had died.

"If you talked to her this morning then you know as much as I do," Amy told him, eager to avoid the subject of sacred music. "She's got one doozy of a case of the flu. My dad didn't think she should be left alone, so he asked me to bring the kids up here."

Adam nodded. "For which we are all exceedingly grateful."

Amy only felt lukewarm about doing Kay a favor, but she had to admit that she would have driven triple the distance in half the time for even a smidgen of Adam Reed's gratitude. Trying to shield her inner glow from his intent gaze, she tossed out, "Fortunately I'm on vacation till September, and I know the route up here like the back of my hand."

He smiled again, a warm, heart-soothing smile that she couldn't believe he would have given to just anybody. "She told me that, too. She said there wasn't a soul alive who loved Camp Colina more than you."

A great ache pierced her midsection as Amy stiffened even in the face of his smile. "Kay is somewhat prone to hyperbole. I came here a few times as a kid. That's all."

She hated the words as soon as they slid off her tongue. It didn't matter that Camp Colina was only a place; it was a sacred place, the place where God had always lived in her childhood memories, and to belittle her love for the camp belittled her love for the Lord. *Well, I've hardly gone out of my way to honor Him lately, have I?* she chided herself, struggling for honesty. "I . . . I really enjoyed this place when I was younger," she backpedaled a bit. "I just meant that . . . it was a long time ago."

Adam's blue eyes searched hers briefly before he whispered, "I knew what you meant."

For a naked moment she was sure that he knew exactly what she meant, even though she still hadn't said it. She didn't want Adam Reed to think badly of her; didn't want this engaging, utterly Christian man to see inside her troubled soul. She was battling for light, meaningless words to fill the space between them when the kids fell back upon them with glee.

"Let's go, Amy!" Joey shouted, less than a foot from her ear. At the same time one of the counselors called to Adam, and the moment between them was effectively destroyed.

"You guys get settled in. I'll see you at supper," he promised, tossing another round of smiles at the children before he melted into the hubbub. But he took only half a dozen paces before he stopped and turned around, his eyes on Amy. For just a moment those compelling blue eyes rested on her face, promising her—promising himself?—that in spite of the chaos, he would get back to her tonight. Then he trotted into the lodge and disappeared from view.

A part of Amy wanted to call after him, *I wish I could see you at supper, too. I wish I could have told you what I'm really feeling. I wish I could see your dazzling smile whenever I'm feeling down. . . .*

But of course she could say none of these things, so she herded the children toward the nearest cabin that Adam had mentioned. Amy was pleased that Grizzly, Joey's home for the next seven days, was right next to the lodge. The less isolated he was the longer it would take him to realize that he was really on his own. She desperately hoped that his counselor would turn out to be a man of Adam Reed's integrity.

Integrity. The word arrowed into her mind and lodged there. It was a characteristic that was painted in bold stripes all over the camp director; a characteristic in scant supply among so many young men nowadays . . . including the one who now surveyed her from the top step of Grizzly Cabin.

"Weeelll . . . hello there!" a cocky male voice hailed her as she approached Joey's erstwhile home. The speaker was broad-chested, regally handsome and bold in his appraisal of Amy's cutoff-clad legs. She was surrounded by an entourage of children, two of them boys who might well have been assigned to his cabin, but the slick stranger on the porch had eyes only for the lovely young woman before him. He wore beige double knit slacks, a white short-sleeved shirt and a pair of Adidas that had never touched the ground. Nice clothes for a working man, but a naked brand of inexperience in the mountains.

A shiver of disappointment trailed down Amy's back. As a male model or an actor this dark-haired and golf course-tanned specimen might have won her applause, if not her respect. But as the care giver of her little brother on his first sojourn to church camp, he left a little to be desired.

"Hello," she replied with a cool gray stare. "This is Joey . . . Shelby." She stumbled over the last name

16

that she knew the boy used even though it would be months before his legal adoption as her father's son. Yet her hand went out protectively to her little brother's shoulder. "He's assigned to Grizzly Cabin."

By this time Joey's face was wreathed in delirious excitement. *Don't disappointment him,* her heart commanded this bold stranger. *If he doesn't have a good time here all my upheaval will be for nothing.*

Reading her message with a "maybe later" glance in reply, the man dropped his gaze to Joey. "Howdy, partner," he declared in a clumsy imitation of Adam Reed's unrehearsed finesse. "I'm Trevor Grant and we'll be bunking together. You want to look around inside?"

"Yes, that would be nice," Amy answered for Joey, quick to include herself in the invitation before Trevor tried to separate her from the children. She sidestepped his muscular bulk, noting with satisfaction that he had a bit of a spare tire growing around his middle. Ignoring him for the moment, Amy followed the children into the cabin, letting them savor the special feeling of Camp Colina's tiny wooden homes.

Knotty pine enclosed the three sides of Grizzly that were nearest the meadow, but the mountain served as the only wall for the back of the cabin. A couple of two by fours served as a railing. Twelve bunks filled the single room; one corner contained a small bathroom. It had been seven years since Amy had last showered in one of these cabins, but she could still feel that icy water on her skin! She could also remember how fresh the evening air was at the fireside bowl, how crisp the dawn breeze as they gathered in the meadow for morning watch. . . .

"Boy, am I relieved to see you," Trevor announced from behind her. "Most of these people are middle aged and decidedly married. I'd given up hope of finding a single counselor with time on her hands."

Amy shook her head. "Sorry. You're out of luck." *Even if I were staying.*

"Alas!" he moaned, laying his right hand on his heart. "A happily married mother of two point three children with a linebacker hubby unloading the car?"

This time his smile almost reached her, and it occurred to Amy that he really was trying to be friendly. He honestly didn't know how to relate to a woman any other way.

"Wrong again," she answered a little more kindly. "I'm just a shirttail relation drafted on a mission of mercy."

Suddenly Joey was beside her asking, "What's a shirttail relation?" His eyes were bright as he waited for her reply.

Fighting the unwelcome sense of shame that swept her, Amy gave him a quick pat on the shoulder and turned back to Trevor. "I've got two more eaglets to place in their nests before I go, but I'll bring up the rest of Joey's things before your group has to go to dinner. I know Irene waits for no man, woman, or child."

The last words brought a smile to Amy's lips as she remembered "Irene the Queen." A tiny woman of enormous strength and gruff Christian cheer, she was as much a part of Camp Colina as the open meadow or the midnight coyote serenade. Her husband, Orville, was the devout lay leader who had directed the camp during most of Amy's youth. He was a small, round man with big, round glasses, and most of the kids had secretly referred to him as "Orville the Owl." Amy remembered that the couple had owned a business in a small college community that turned into a ghost town every June, so the permanent summer jobs fit perfectly into their lives. They had always spoken of Camp Colina as their second home; the possibility that they were no loner here was untenable.

"Irene?" Trevor repeated blankly, confirming his status as a newcomer to the camp.

18

"The cook. I think . . . I hope?"

He shook his head. "Beats me. I've only been here a couple of hours myself. I'm not sure if I'll survive the food if it's anything like the Army."

"It's not." Her defense surprised her. But Irene wasn't here to defend herself—maybe wasn't even at the camp at all any more—and this stranger had no right to belittle her cooking. *Or my wonderful childhood memories. . . .*

"You've been in the Army?" he asked, cocking an eyebrow in disbelief.

"Of course not. But I've been eating Irene's cooking every summer since I was Joey's age, and it's always been wonderful." *Why did I leave out the last seven years? Why did I make it sound like Camp Colina is still part of my life?*

Trevor looked relieved. "I'm glad to hear it. The last time I was at a Bible camp the food was as dry as the preaching." Missing the cues of Amy's obvious discomfort, he went on, "My mother kept sending us every summer. She kept hoping we'd all 'get religion.'"

"I take it you didn't," Amy retorted sharply. *I didn't really say that!* she heard her mind echo. But she was already feeling pretty defensive today, and she would have been offended by his attitude anyway. Her own religious standing was a bit questionable at the moment, but it wasn't because she didn't believe in God. She was just afraid that *He* no longer believed in *her*.

Deciding not to apologize under the circumstances, Amy told him, "Why are you up here if you feel so . . . so. . . ."

"Out of place?" he grinned, unrepentant. "Good question." Suddenly the levity faded from his voice as he met her eyes, cool and unimpressed with his phony bravado. Pretense slipped from his shoulders like a tuxedo after a wedding. "The simple truth is that I

19

haven't seen my daughter in some time and I felt the need of a . . . well, a friendly backdrop while we got reacquainted. I didn't want us to spend this first week staring at the T.V. while we tried not to stare at each other." He almost looked embarrassed. "I guess I'm . . . afraid to be alone with Tiffany just yet."

Amy was silent, touched by the blunt confession. How quickly she'd discarded this glib man as shallow and uncaring! He wore an unappealing mask, but obviously there was another side of Trevor Grant that he was not eager to show the world. Yet she wondered if he were telling her the whole truth about his daughter. Was Tiffany just a good cover for his own struggling Christianity? Maybe he really wanted to be here.

Just like me. Again she stopped herself. She didn't want to be at Camp Colina; it made her nervous. Too many well-buried feelings were struggling to find their way out of her heart. She wouldn't last another hour in this place without a good cry.

"Well, I hope you all have a good week," she announced to nobody in particular. "I've got to get Cindy and Nathan settled in before I start back down the mountain."

Instantly Trevor was alert. "You're not going before supper, are you?" he looked almost childishly eager. "The dinner gong will ring in less than half an hour. Besides, after that big speech you just gave me, you must be dying to check out Irene's cooking."

Amy smiled courteously but shook her head. "I have a long way to go." *In more ways than one*.

"So do I," he answered quietly. Amy met his eyes for just a second, wondering what secret torment had driven him away from his daughter . . . his God? She wanted to tell him she would pray for him, but she didn't think she could.

"I'm sorry . . . for what I said about the Bible camp," he muttered. "If I didn't have good memories

20

I don't think I would have ended up here this week. I just . . . wanted to impress you, I guess, and most of the women I've been seeing lately are turned off by too much religion."

Amy met his eyes squarely. "Most women are turned off by a man who doesn't have the courage to express own his beliefs in public, no matter what they are." She shook her head. What a strange place this camp was! Instant intimacy . . . blunt pronouncements . . . spiritual memories that nobody could ever take away.

Get out of here, Amy. Before the spell catches you. . . .

"I've got to go. I hope . . . I hope this week gives you and your daughter what you need, Trevor," she told him sincerely.

He nodded, looking a bit embarrassed, then said goodbye as Amy marched out the door, promising Joey she'd return with his things.

"Who's next?" Nathan asked her, his freckle-faced grin showing new animation.

"Umm . . . you are, I think." She looked up as they passed Timber Wolf, the cabin Kay had been assigned to. Idly she wondered who Adam had found to take over for her. Cheerful young squeals rose from within, but the quiet voice of a mature woman also hinted of adequate control.

The next cabin was Cottontail, where Amy had stayed the first time she'd ever sung a solo for the closing night service. She ushered Nathan inside, delivering him to a balding gentleman with a Mr. Rogers smile and a wedding ring prominently displayed on his left hand.

"Mark Ferris," he greeted her cheerfully, "but at camp they call me 'Grand Slam.' Silly, I know, but everybody gets labeled with some nickname up here. It could have been worse." He greeted the twins and kept up a cheerful prattle. "My wife and I have six

21

kids and fourteen grandchildren, but we can't seem to get enough, so we come up here for a week every summer. Her name's Marilyn—Pinky up here, I forget why—and she's over in Eagle. If you've got any more stuff, Nathan, I'll help you get settled. Dinner's coming up and we sure don't want to be late!'' He patted his rotund middle and winked at Amy. She said goodbye, knowing that Nathan was in good hands, then quickly delivered Cindy to an equally cheerful and competent counselor on the other side of the camp.

She should have gone directly to the car, hustled out Joey's things and disappeared down the dusty trail before darkness and dinner entrapped her here. She wanted to tell Adam to keep a special eye out for Joey, especially in view of her less than reassuring meeting with his counselor. But she couldn't be absolutely sure that Joey was her only motivation for wanting to talk to Adam again, and he was still knee deep in little people up at the lodge and surely had a million things to do.

For some reason that she could not explain, even to herself, she needed to tour the rest of the camp before she left. Using the old shortcut through the pines, she headed toward the fireside bowl on the north side of the camp. It had always been a special place for Amy, and new memories stirred as she first reached the crest where it came into view. Communion with homebaked bread and a clay jar; sermons by camp counselors and lay leaders, quiet prayers by jean-clad pastors; music from tiny voices, infused, somehow, with a special grace. A thorn of loss scratched her heart; a curious jealousy plagued her as she realized that Joey would now have this peace from her childhood, just as he now had her father's love. She was tempted to sit on the rough hewn logs and make the effort—this one last time—to pray. If she could do it anywhere, it would be here.

22

For a long parade of minutes Amy sat perfectly still before a blue jay shrieked, mocking her futile desire for forgiveness. Abruptly she thought of Orville the Owl, and realized that if Adam had replaced him then someone else had surely replaced Irene. It wasn't really the same place at all. She sighed deeply and left the bowl.

Reluctantly she wandered back past the swimming pool and the Canteen, where cokes, stamps and that ever-present plastic cord for making necklaces and dog leashes could be purchased each afternoon after the camp nap. It had been a special time. *But it's in the past, Amy.* Faith, like childhood, was something she seemed to have outgrown.

It was Joey's turn now. It was time for her to collect his things, say goodbye, and take just a moment to mention his needs to Adam Reed. But first . . . first, there was one more place she had to go. Just one more song to sing.

CHAPTER 2

THE TRAIL TO THE CHAPEL was steep and full of rocks. Half way up the hillside there was a trickling creek that some early camper had dubbed the "Jordan River." Because the chapel was an enclosed building—primitive, but nonetheless enclosed—it was never used in the summer unless there was an unseasonal rainstorm or other natural calamity. As a result, when services were held on the top of the hill campers declared that it was time to "cross the Jordan," a physical as well as spiritual journey of no small dimensions. Amy was breathing hard by the time she reached the rustic cross that pierced the skyline.

She could not pretend that it was random chance that had brought her to this oak-hewn relic, this casual, timeless house of worship. She needed to be here, needed to relive the spiritual memories that had uplifted her . . . needed to ask the old joy to rub against the new pain until she had a chance of feeling whole again.

Her eye noted with satisfaction that the massive

granite fireplace had not changed; it still dominated the front of the chapel. A manzanita branch, big enough to be called a tree, served as a centerpiece over the mantle. At Christmas, she remembered, they put tiny lights on it because no one in these mountains would cut down a free-growing tree. Hanging from the ceiling, between a handcarved pulpit and even more rustic lectern, was a cross made of two slim pine trunks, with the bark still attached.

There were no normal chairs or pews in the room. Unattached tree stumps were scattered here and there in a formation too vague to be designated as rows. One or two side tables made of redwood allowed for placement of communion or candles. A bookcase held a tiny collection of camp hymnals and tattered Bibles. Nothing had changed.

And then she saw it. Pushed unobtrusively into a distant corner that virtually served as a closet, covered with a dusty Mexican sarape, its mildewed, hiking boot-scuffed legs carving holes in the shifting camp top soil, leaned the piano. Not just any piano: *the* piano of the summer after her senior year. Had it waited here all this time, buried in this dusty corner, to rise up like a Phoenix from the ashes, eager to haunt her like a cross engraved with her own private name?

"Dear God," she whispered, unaware that her lips framed a prayer, "Will you spare me nothing?"

She wanted to run, to hide from this heirloom of maternal love and family closeness. But her mother's memory, ever patient, ever warm, called to her, embedded in the ancient piano like a spirit in a grave. Cautiously she approached the piano, her fingers aching to heal the broken, dirty keys. The lid was open; no one had even bothered to shelter the loyal old music maker from aging. Amy's hands swept back the sarape, gripped the black wood music stand, then slowly melted lower until her fingers touched the keys.

Slowly, mesmerized, she ran her hands over the keyboard in a quick set of scales. Her touch was sure and light. The poor old thing was pathetically out of tune, but it had suffered no irreparable damage in its years of patent neglect.

Amy felt a stir of anger at Adam Reed. He was in charge of every aspect of the camp. Had he no respect for music? The piano was no great classic, but it did its best. In its sweet and simple way it had called more youngsters to Christ than the fifteen-rank custom built organ that Kay played every Sunday morning.

It was suddenly more than Amy could bear. She found a fairly high redwood stump-stool and tucked it under the keyboard. Grabbing a discarded sweat shirt from the floor, she dusted down the keys. At least her fingers wouldn't slosh around in the dirt!

And then she waited for a song to come to her hands. One of the dozens and dozens that she'd loved and learned in this majestic holy place. One of the musical tools of the Gardener who bent eager young twigs who sought Him at Camp Colina. One of the multitudinous repertoire of Christian hymns and anthems that had lived in her fingertips and heart for years and years until the last time she'd stood in the Lord's shadow and reached for His sun . . . His *Son*. The day they laid her mother in the ground.

There was only one song for her mother that day . . . just as there had been only one song for her mother the last time they came to camp as a family; one song for her daughter to sing, her mother to accompany, on this tired but ever faithful camp-church piano. Only one song she could play for her now.

It took a whole verse, plodded out with frighteningly uncertain fingers, before she dared to sing the words.

Amazing grace; how sweet the sound,
That saved a wretch like me!

26

I once was lost, but now I'm found;
Was blind, but now I see!

She sang the same verse three times before she could remember what came next. The words—The Word—had been hidden so long inside her that they battled with grief and guilt to rise from her mouth. She lost all contact with her place in this empty, dusty room; all awareness that with darkness coming on the massive bell would ring, calling two hundred tiny "Christianettes" to supper. She didn't notice that daylight had subsided so greatly that she was all but playing in the dark. She did not notice the tall, quiet man with compassionate blue eyes who heard her voice from the path outside and walked silently into the room to stand behind her.

'Twas grace that taught me heart to fear,
And grace my fears relieved;
How precious did that grace appear
The hour I first believed!

She made it through three and a half verses, her voice ringing out with all of its pain and beauty, before her will power shattered . . . her fractured soul rewounded . . . as she collapsed on the keyboard with her head pressed against her hands. The tears broke forth from their long guarded hiding place, sweeping over her reddened cheeks like a river that's jumped its dam.

She spoke not a word. But inside she raged at Kay for sending her here, raged at God for taking her mother, raged at herself for her adolescent loss of values. How desperately she wished she could turn to Jesus for comfort! But she had lost Him when she'd turned her back on her mother. She'd buried them together that terrible November day.

At first she thought it was the Hand of God that touched her shoulder—a desperate vision of her imagination?—and she looked up only to make sure she hadn't imagined hope where there was none. When she saw the face of a human being mirroring every quiver of her anguish, she screamed. It was an involuntary response. She was stunned, disappointed and acutely embarrassed. Adam Reed was the last person to whom she wanted to explain herself. She jerked away from him, her trembling hands tugging the sarape over the keyboard in a futile gesture of despair.

"I'm sorry . . . Miss Shelby . . . truly, I didn't mean to frighten you. I thought you heard me come in. I've been standing—" He cut off as though he realized it would not comfort her to know how much of her privacy he'd inadvertently invaded.

"Please go away," she breathed, feeling like he'd taken a machete and carved open her soul. Why? Was it just the nearness of a stranger who was witnessing her grief? Or was it the sense of perfect communion, as though he knew every ache in her heart without a word? She could see it! Her own grief in his eyes! How could he know?

"Miss Shelby," he started again, his voice low and somber, cautiously warm, "Your voice was so exquisite . . . so full of tortured grace . . . I had to listen. I had to be here. Now I know why." He paused to read her mute resistance, but after a moment he pressed on. "Please let me help you. You don't have to hurt this much alone."

"Yes I do!" she whispered fiercely, still struggling for her normal voice. "This cross has my name on it. It's the punishment He gave me when she died." He didn't ask what she meant. It was as though he understood. "I know it must seem that way at times. But if you're a Christian, you know that God doesn't punish people for their shortcomings. He forgives everything; He helps them learn from their mistakes; he sends messengers of love to draw out the poison of pain and—"

"I'm not . . . I mean . . . I don't know if I'm a Christian anymore." The words came out in a sob. "It's not that I . . . don't want to be. It's that . . . I can't seem to find a pew with my name on it."

Very carefully, he smiled. It brought out the warmth in his sea blue eyes and the sunny laugh lines that graced his sun-blond temples. "I think I can help you find your pew, Miss Shelby. And I promise you that your name is still legible under the dust." He did not sound pious as he quoted simply, " 'I have engraved you on the palms of my hands.' "

One part of Amy that she'd forgotten replied, "Isaiah 49 . . . verse 16 or 17, if I'm not mistaken."

This time his smile grew, stroking her with its uncomplicated warmth and decency. "Close enough."

A grin on her own face surprised her, struggling to respond to the man in spite of her grief. "Aren't you going to tell me which verse it is?"

He laughed. A rich, baritone ring that told her all was right with the world. "You've got to be kidding. And snatch away from you the moment when you're utterly ripe to pick up a Bible again . . . even if it is just for curiosity's sake?"

On that note he turned and headed for the book-case, plucking out one of the faithful servants. He held it toward her, then set it back on the pile. "I can't read it for you," he said simply. "But it will be here waiting for you always." He headed for the door. Then he paused, reading the quiet look of panic in her eyes. "Believe me, Miss Shelby, I'd never leave you here alone."

When he was gone, his spirit lingered. The peace he brought stayed with her.

At least fifteen minutes passed before Amy left the chapel and started down the hill toward the meadow. The dinner bell had already issued its imperious

29

summons, and she knew the only course open to her was to deliver Joey's things and then join him at the lodge.

The long, outdoor tables had not changed in her absence; neither had the herd of yellow jackets that blanketed the red and white checked table cloths and colorless tableware. It was strange how such diverse creatures—humans and stinging insects—managed to live so peaceably side by side. But the yellow jackets were as much a part of her Camp Colina memory as was Pillsie, the crusty nurse who'd been there every summer. They both looked terribly threatening but never harmed a soul.

She couldn't say the same for the rattlesnakes and coyotes that roamed the outer reaches of the camp hills. More than one rattler had been killed in the main part of the camp during high summer. The coyotes, of course, joined the singing every night from a respectful distance. As a general rule, they kept to their own territory . . . dens by day, hiking trails only at night. It was a system that seemed to work unless somebody broke the rules.

"Over here," Joey hollered at her from his perch on a bench several tables to her left. She nodded absently, amazed at his unabashed enthusiasm. Not for the camp—it had always affected her in the same way. What she couldn't understand was how he could be so fond of *her*. She'd avoided going home as much as possible since her father's remarriage, and had virtually ignored this child on the few occasions she'd been forced to go. Yet he treated her like royalty. Shame wrapped itself around her like a hairshirt.

"How's your cabin, Joey?" she asked, eager to show some interest. "Have you made some new friends?"

"Sure!" he all but bubbled. "That's Jeffrey over there . . . ," he pointed toward a giggling towhead, " . . . and Roger next to the Giraffe."

"The Giraffe?" Amy asked, observing that Trevor Grant was sitting next to the boy in question.

"Sure. All the other counselors already gots nicknames, so we made one up for him." Joey gave her a wrinkle-nosed smile that tugged at her heart. "Don't you like it?"

She smiled at Joey, then at Trevor, who looked a little bit embarrassed. "I think it's very . . . distinguished."

The other boys at the table joined in Joey's laughter before he asked Amy, "I wonder what we ought to nickname you? You don't look funny or wear weird clothes. All you do is carry your guitar wherever you go—"

"Joey, the nicknames are only for counselors," she told him quietly. But he'd moved on to other conversation by then and didn't seem to hear. It was just as well. Amy had thoughts of her own to clear.

Adam had just entered from the meadow, hailing folks right and left as he wove a trail to the head table. He looked less somber now—an image of good will and constant cheer. She wondered what he thought about their strange encounter. It wasn't as though he'd tried to force the Bible on her; he'd offered it as a gift, a gift he thought she needed, a gift—she had to admit deep within her—that *she* thought she needed, too.

For a long, quiet space of time after he'd left her she'd stared at that dusty Bible, waiting for it to open, or cross the room to her. But it hadn't been that easy, and not even her curiosity about Isaiah had been enough to propel her toward those ancient pages. Now, paradoxically, she regretted her cowardice.

"Amy. Amy!" Joey was tugging on her sleeve. "You aren't listening! What are you thinking about, anyway?"

Feeling somewhat disjointed, she turned to study her new brother and blurted out, "I was wondering

31

where I'd left my Bible." Not the only one she'd ever owned . . . just the most important. The one her mother had given her the day she joined the church.

"Oh, it's okay, Amy!" Joey promised brightly. "You can borrow mine until you get unpacked. I can't read it too good anyway."

Amy felt the tug again. What was it about this place? She'd felt more despair and shattering hope in the last half hour than she'd felt in the last two years. She had to get out of here before she came apart all together. Maybe she could make a donation to get the piano tuned. . . .

"Glad to see you decided to stay for dinner, Amy," Trevor told her with a cautious smile.

"It seemed like the thing to do." She knew she sounded stilted, but she wasn't sure she wanted to encourage this confused searcher . . . especially when her thoughts were full of another man.

"I hate to tell you this, but Irene isn't here anymore. At least, she's not the cook. I asked. Apparently she lives in some remodeled groundskeeper's cabin up on one of these mountains aptly named 'Persistence Peak.'" He said it as though he thought poor Irene couldn't find anywhere else to live. "Apparently her husband was the camp director here before Adam Reed and the powers that be gave him permission to fix up the cabin when he retired."

Amy smiled. How well she remembered the summit Trevor had mentioned! "I'm glad. That's exactly where the two of them should be." Before Trevor could respond, a sing-song cry began to sweep over the tables.

"Announcements, announcements, annou . . . ounce . . . ments!"

The musical tones, unchanged by years of Christian campers, flickered over the group, embellished by eager young voices as the message took root. The tiny verse had been repeated maybe four times before

32

everyone stopped talking and faced the head table, where Adam stood, regally banging on a ceramic mug with his spoon.

Amy was afraid to meet his eyes, so she looked around the gathering instead. The children were pretty much seated according to cabin assignments, with one grownup at every table. One of them Amy recognized—Pillsie, the gruff and pudgy nurse from her childhood. What a comfort to see a familiar face! The elderly woman was sitting with one group of little girls, causing Amy to wonder who their counselor was. It suddenly occurred to her that Pillsie might be filling in for Kay. She was surprised that her stepmother's replacement hadn't arrived yet.

"Good evening everybody, and welcome to Camp Colina," Adam began brightly. "I know you're all starving so I'll be brief. After dinner we'll all be meeting down at the bowl for worship, just as soon as the lucky cabins who drew kitchen duty tonight are done with the dishes." He checked his list. "That's Timber Wolf and Grizzly." The counselors laughed, and several kids groaned.

"That's me, huh?" Joey asked her.

Before she could answer Adam continued his speech.

"But right now, before we sing grace, I'd like to make sure that everybody knows who the counselors are, just in case some of you came in late and aren't real sure just where you ought to be. I'm in charge of the camp this summer, so you can come to me anytime. I don't have a regular cabin . . . my room's in the back of the lodge. My real name's Adam Reed, but at camp they call me 'Summit.' "

The kids giggled even though they probably didn't know what the nickname meant. Amy wasn't sure herself. He was tall enough to be named for a mountain, but he might also have mastered a difficult peak . . . on the camp grounds or even in his personal

33

life. She didn't have much time to ponder this as he quickly introduced each counselor by his or her cabin assignment and nickname. It was no surprise to Amy that Pinky Ferris was just as outgoing as her husband, or that two or three of the other counselors were also regulars who returned to Camp Colina every year.

There were nine women and ten men altogether, not counting Adam and Amy. She was just beginning to wonder why he hadn't mentioned Kay when out of nowhere he beamed at her, tossed a welcoming hand in her direction, and announced in a voice that brimmed with confidence, "And last but certainly not least let me introduce our noble last minute volunteer, the lovely young lady in charge of the lucky dishwashing group at Timber Wolf Cabin tonight, a special person who'll put a song in all our hearts: 'Amos' Shelby!"

He grinned at Amy as though he expected her to be flattered or pleased by his glorious introduction. The dimpled smile never faded, even while he waited for her to stand, waited for her to smile, waited for her to move from the trance of frozen rage—or was it fear?—that had seized her the instant her name left his lips.

"Amy," Trevor whispered from across the table, "you need to stand up or wave."

She held up one hand. The expression on her face never wavered, even when the rest of the group began to clap and cheer. Fortunately the applause dissolved as soon as Adam announced that dinner was getting cold, but by then Amy had begun to realize the corner he had maneuvered her into.

"I thought you said you weren't staying," Trevor said.

"I'm not."

He glanced from Amy to Adam and back again. "I wouldn't lay any bets on that. Adam obviously wants you here."

For no reason at all Amy's heart did a quick flip on the balance beam of her ribs, clattering awkwardly back to its rightful position as she reminded herself sternly, *Any interest in that man has in you is purely spiritual. You must have imagined that first moment when you met. . . .*

Belatedly she realized that Trevor was watching her with a penetrating gaze. How much did he see? With mock eagerness she attacked her spaghetti, which a few moments ago she had been more than happy to eat. But now it was hard to get down a single mouthful . . . and not because it wasn't quite as good as Irene's. Adam's words clogged her throat. How dare he! For all that tender compassion there was a man of steel embedded in that lanky frame. Adam Reed had decided that she needed to stay at this camp, and one way or another he'd make sure that she did.

It was all Kay's fault, really. If only she hadn't promised to do this . . . if only she hadn't gotten sick. . . . Slowly it came to Amy that maybe Adam really *did* think she was replacing Kay! After all, she had brought the kids up here and she certainly hadn't jumped right up and told him he was wrong when he'd called her "Amos." And she still wasn't sure why.

Was it because of those few sweet moments when a perfect stranger had tried to ease her grief . . . a stranger she was undeniably attracted to? Was it because of the eager young faces that were starting to crowd around her, expecting her to be their mother, father, teacher and big sister for the week? Was it the glowing mask of pride on Joey's face? Or was it possibly a niggling sense that maybe she'd like to spend a week at Camp Colina after all?

She brushed away the last thought as she stood in line to empty her plate, then marched stoically to Adam's table.

"I need to speak to you privately," she declared as calmly as she could.

"Sure thing, Amos," he replied genially, taking another piece of garlic bread from the hot metal plate. "How about right after the service?"

"No," she sizzled, losing control in the face of his willful denseness. "I need to talk to you right now."

His eyes narrowed playfully. "Ah. You don't like tonight's duty roster, is that it? Tsk, tsk, Amos. There's two hundred plates and glasses waiting for you."

"There's also a car waiting for me at the base of the hill," she forced out in a terse whisper, unable to keep the anger out of her voice.

He got it then. Alarm grew in those deep blue eyes that swept over Amy, then went on to embrace the handful of little girls who trailed her in silent waiting. Suddenly she was ashamed. There were six of them already, blue jeaned and bright and increasingly uneasy as she failed to reassure them. One of them stared at her sullenly, twisting her blond hair in tight little knots as she waited for her counselor to acknowledge her.

Amy turned back to Adam, who was moving quickly around the table until he reached her side. He took her arm companionably, as though to reassure her, but she knew he was sending a silent plea for help. Reluctantly she found her voice.

"If you girls will go into the kitchen and tell the cook you're on K.P. duty, she'll tell you what to do. When you're done go on down to the bowl." She pointed across the meadow, then sighed as her tiny troopers scampered away. She hadn't forgotten the drill.

She looked up as Adam released her arm. Abject gratitude filled his face. Without a word he tossed his head in the direction of the lodge. She followed mutely.

Adam led her into his office, a tiny room with an old wooden desk and a couple of chairs. One entire wall

36

was filled with books. Some of them were inspirational and some were light fiction. One entire section dealt
with Biblical research, and a pile on his desk consisted of practical camp manuals. Amy wished she'd had
the time to examine his entire library. What secrets of
the man it would unveil!

"Please sit down, Amos." The somber tone of his
voice almost mitigated the response she had to the
name. Almost.

"I'm not one of your counselors, Adam, so you can
drop the silly nickname," she declared acerbically,
plopping down in a chair across from the desk.
Against her will her eye flitted toward the well-worn
Bible that lay on the nearest corner. Gold letters on
the cover spelled out Adam's name.

"I'm truly sorry if the name offends you, Miss
Shelby," he told her gravely. "The simple truth is, I
can't recall your first name. I had to come up with
something."

Amy wasn't sure how to respond. How could a man
who read her very soul manage to forget her name?
Yet she had to admit that there had been a change in
the way Adam treated her since their strange communion in the chapel. Despite his Christian warmth
and caring, that man-woman promise of their first
meeting had not flickered between them since he'd
heard her first notes on the piano. Had she rendered
herself ineligible for a relationship with this man when
she'd admitted the inadequacy of her broken faith? Or
was he keeping this new distance between them for
some other reason? Trying to find her way out of a
tornado of feelings, Amy fenced, "You're going to tell
me that 'Amos' isn't a camp spinoff of Amy?"

He smiled. Very carefully. "Perhaps a seed of
memory lurked in my mind. But actually I chose your
nickname for entirely Biblical reasons."

She stiffened. Against her will she glanced down at
his Bible, trying desperately to remember which story

37

belonged to Amos. Old Testament, somewhere between Psalms and the end. Not the one with the whale . . . that was Jonah. Not the one who faced the lions . . . that was Daniel. With swirling curiosity she met his eyes. Their intensity surprised her. He was willing her . . . *begging* her to reach for that Bible!

Suddenly she laughed. How silly and stubborn she must seem to him! "Oh Adam, I'm sorry. I'm just not ready yet."

His blue eyes warmed, withholding judgment. "I know that, Amos. But you're very close, I think." He nodded, as if to confirm his own pronouncement. "I hope you won't be too proud to share the good news with me when it happens."

She should have bristled at those words, but she didn't. Instead she was touched that such a devout Christian cared so much for her dormant faith. And pleased that she had a reason to write to Adam. When he reached out to take her hand, she seized his and returned the squeeze. "I will, Adam," she found herself saying. "I'll drop you a note."

He released her with a smile. "Unless you're still here."

Her eyes opened a shade wider. "I won't be here, Adam. I thought you understood by now—I agreed to drive the kids up here. That's all."

He leaned back in his wooden chair, bracing it on two legs. "I'm getting that, Amos." His eyes floated over her face, searching for something she couldn't quite place. "The simple truth is, I don't know what to do about it."

She stood up, feeling the noose tighten. "Then I'll tell you what to do about it. Say, 'Thanks for the music, Amy. I hope you find God.' Then say, 'Goodbye.'"

But Adam said nothing. Instead his eyes pinned hers, waiting, reminding her of the ten little girls doing dishes without her, who had nobody else to lead them. In her own mind she saw Joey, his eager pride a source for her ongoing shame. And then there was her father, who would have expected her to fill in this way. *If Kay were my mother, she wouldn't have had to ask. Of course I'd fill in.*

"I don't even have any clothes with me. Somebody would have to feed my cat—"

"Amos," he interrupted gently, ignoring her paper stonewalling, "It's already dark. This is no time to be starting out for anywhere in a car. In a pinch I could send the nurse back up to Timber Wolf, but she's got too much work to do already. I haven't any idea where I'd scrape up another counselor on such short notice, and even if I could, I'm not sure I could improve on you. Kay sings your praises; she says you work with children and know this camp like the back of your hand. Your ministry of music alone could—"

"I don't have a ministry of music!" she burst out shrilly. "I don't play Christian music anymore."

Again their eyes met tensely. In the silence they could both hear her earlier haunted strains of "Amazing Grace." Adam's voice dropped to a whisper as he told her, "You need to be here right now, Amy Shelby. If the only job I had open was room and board for dusting off the trees, I'd try to get you to stay. You're so close, so terribly close. Please don't run away now. You just don't have to go on hurting."

Amy turned away, jamming her hands in her pockets like a ten-year-old child. "You have no right to press me like this. You don't have any idea what I've done or why this is so hard for me." She whipped back to face him. "You're not a musician, are you?"

He shook his head. "But I always try to 'make a joyful noise unto the Lord' just the same."

"I can't be joyful here, Adam. I can't make music and I can't go down to the bowl for worship. Every time I've tried to go to church in the last seven years I—"

39

She broke off, stunned that she'd already revealed so much. Yet it seemed natural to bare her soul to Adam. He seemed to understand her better than she understood herself. She was almost ready to share a little bit more of her grief when Adam's voice, low and in prayer, broke through her reverie.

"Lord, please join us here in this hour before dawn. Help this special person to turn her face toward your great light. Cleanse her wounds and heal the source of pain within her. Surround her with your infinite forgiveness. Let her know how eagerly you wait for her."

And then the tone of prayer changed. "Heavenly Father, please be at my side tonight as I lead these children in their first experience at camp prayer. Help me in this new assignment you have chosen for me. Strengthen those who have volunteered to serve the children, and give me the wisdom to lead them all toward their greatest calling. Amen."

She felt empty, broken, by his quiet prayer. With the children he exuded confidence, yet only to his Maker—and to her—had he revealed his insecurity. Or was it just another ploy?

"You really play hardball, Adam Reed," she whispered, refusing to meet his eyes.

He sighed. A tired sound, laced with despair. "There's nothing else I can do for you, Amy. I'll take the girls up to Timber Wolf after the service. If you're not there, I'll make other arrangements." He moved around the desk and stood beside her. She could feel his presence aching to heal her. She could not look at him.

"God bless you on your journey, Amos, wherever it may lead," he breathed against her hair. Then he briskly marched away, his stride sure and certain as he marched down the hall. She could hear every footstep as clearly as a striking gong in a steeple until he reached the dirt trail outside the building. Then

pine needles cushioned his tracks until only a whisper
of his voice lingered in her ears.

CHAPTER 3

AFTER ADAM LEFT Amy had no idea what she really wanted to do. She only knew that she had never felt lonelier in her life. And then she realized, with a sudden burst of inescapable clarity, that if she couldn't cure the loneliness at Camp Colina, she couldn't cure it anywhere.

It was a surprising discovery. Up till this moment, she hadn't even known she was lonely. Basically Amy was a cheerful, efficient person with many close friends and a solid relationship with her family. Of course, the family had changed radically since her father had married Kay, and in her more truthful moments, Amy had to admit that most of the adjustment problems were hers. A vision of Joey flashed before her eyes—wagging his tail with eagerness and pride when he'd introduced his big sister. He had no idea she'd planned to leave him here. Suddenly she didn't ever want him to know.

Joey's offer to loan her his Bible scratched at the edge of her consciousness, right next door to the place where Adam kept scattering Biblical clues like breadcrumbs in a fairy tale. How Amy longed to unlock the treasures still in storage there for her! As her eyes crept hesitantly toward the Bible that still lay on his desk, she felt an inexpressible longing to clutch it tightly to her chest.

She didn't. But she did reach out, ever so tentatively, to stroke the nubby black cover. Even that felt good; like an itch that could be scratched no other way. She ran one finger down the red-lined side of the sacred pages, savoring the memory of their delicacy.

She knew that Adam would have welcomed her intrusion in his study, would have encouraged her to sit right down and read the Holy Book or take it with her to read under a flashlight in the cabin before she fell asleep . . . or even as a mute companion on the coward's ride back home in the car. But she felt unworthy, somehow . . . not quite ready to take that step. Not quite ready to admit she wanted to stay.

Amy was careful to close the door of the office as she left, threading her way through the dust and twigs to Timber Wolf Cabin, perched high on a rise that overlooked the meadow. The evening air was full of woodsmoke and the sound of children's voices singing in the bowl, sweet but undisciplined as they searched for someone to lead them. Amy shook her head. This was ridiculous. The camp needed her as much as she needed it. Why keep fighting it? Her guitar was in the car . . . and a lifetime of Christian camp songs was stored in her head. As for the piano up at the chapel. . . . She could ignore the chapel. They only gathered up there when the weather was bad anyway.

Amy was still debating her position when she reached Timber Wolf. She had only planned to edge into the empty cabin to see if she could feel at home; but the sight of Kay's name on the door, followed by a list of ten eager little girls, pushed her over the brink of decision. In a burst of determination she took out a pen and crossed off Kay's name and wrote in her own instead.

It was obvious that Pillsie had settled the girls in, for all but one bunk had a sleeping bag laid out and a suitcase or duffle bag stored beneath. Amy had neither, of course, but she had no doubt that Adam would provide her with the rudiments of home once he realized he'd won this round. Deciding to stake her claim, Amy tossed her purse onto the empty mattress and released a great sigh.

"Guess that'll have to do for now, Adam," she declared out loud.

Instantly she heard a bed creak. Against the far wall her eyes pinned the blond girl she'd noticed up at the lodge . . . the hostile hair-twisting tomboy who seemed even more out of place here than Amy did.

"You said Summit was here!" the girl accused her, her voice tense and full of unshed tears.

Trying to control her surprise, Amy said calmly, "I'm sorry if I startled you. I was just talking to myself."

"Well, you can go talk to yourself somewhere else!" Her tone was belligerent, but Amy sensed grief beneath the fire. Quietly she crossed the room, deciding to give the youngster a chance to get her problem off her chest before she became too authoritarian.

"I'm Amy Shelby," she announced. "What's your name?"

The girl pondered the question for a while before she tossed out defiantly, "Tiffany Grant."

"Tiffany!" Amy replied with some enthusiasm, glad she knew something about the child. "I met your father today. He's so excited about spending this week here with you."

Tiffany rolled over, her back slapping both Amy and her father in the face.

In spite of the rebuff, Amy tried to be kind. "If you're assigned to this cabin, Tiffany, I'm your counselor for the week. If there's anything I can help you with—"

44

"There's nothing anyone can help me with. Just leave me alone." Then, almost as an afterthought, she tossed back smugly, "You don't want to be here anyway."

Amy, honest to a fault, did not refute the girl's words. She didn't even question how Tiffany had perceived her own reticence. Instead she declared firmly, "Regardless of why you and I are here, Tiffany, while we live in this cabin—in this camp, for that matter—we are family and we will be kind to each other. Is that understood?"

Tiffany squirmed but did not answer.

"Like I said, any time you need to get something off your chest I'll be happy to listen. But I won't tolerate your rudeness." She said the words without anger, but Tiffany got her point. The girl's mute surrender heartened her. This cabin *did* need somebody experienced with children. Tiffany would have walked all over Kay and spoiled the week for all the other girls! Amy had seen a willful child sour a gathering like this before.

Suddenly she thought of Tiffany's response to Adam's name, and she knew she had nothing to worry about. That man could melt the hardest of hearts!

"Come on, Tiffany," she declared almost brightly. "Let's go."

"Where?" the girl questioned, her voice now more curious than angry.

"To the bowl, of course. We're already late for worship." As she studied the look of baffled relief on the girl's face Amy realized, quite suddenly, that Tiffany had really *wanted* somebody to make her join the group. She was pierced with such a sharp sense of déjà vu that she heard herself muttering, "Some of us are a lot later than others." But she smiled as she headed toward the sound of the voices.

Tiffany did not smile; she did not even speak as she trailed Amy across the meadow, deliberately dawdling

45

just enough to slow her down. Never one to back down from a challenge, Amy tried a new approach.

"Is this your first trip to camp, Tiffany?"

The girl nodded. "And my last, if I can help it."

Amy asked her quite directly, "Why? Why don't you like Camp Colina?"

And Tiffany answered just as bluntly, "Because my dad made me come. I haven't heard from him once since he walked out on me and now he just shows up and decides he's got to be with me or die. How stupid does he think I am?"

Amy had assumed that Trevor and Tiffany's mother were estranged, if not divorced, but something in the way the girl said "walked out on me" made her doubt that she normally lived with her mother . . . even question whether or not her mother was still alive. Of course, it would be instinctive for Amy to assume that a lost mother was at the heart of the young girl's troubles, but at present her problems were clearly centered on her father.

Realizing that she would have to gain Tiffany's trust before she could help her, Amy suggested, "Maybe you should pretend he isn't here at all and just be glad you've got a chance to spend a week at camp."

"Glad?" the girl harrumphed. "It's just as bad as school."

Amy shook her head, knowing she'd taken on a pretty hard case. What had happened to this child? She couldn't be more than seven! She had beautiful, delicate features soured by her frown and awkward gestures. Her blue eyes were haunted; her voice as cynical as a hardened grownup stripped of the zest for life.

"Camp Colina isn't anything like school, Tiffany. I used to come here all the time when I was your age, and I loved it! We got to go hiking and swimming every day, and we made some beautiful things out of beads and leather. And on the last night every cabin

46

performed a skit in the bowl before the service. I always cried when I had to go home."

Her guileless enthusiasm surprised Tiffany. Still she frowned as they padded on the dusty trail to the edge of the bowl.

"I bet you didn't have to go with your father," she fenced.

"Yes, I did. With my mother and father at family camp, and then as a junior camper some years, too. It was very special to all of us."

Suddenly Amy was quiet. She'd gone as far as she could for the moment. Even if she could have given Tiffany her much needed "you'll be so sorry when he's gone" speech, she doubted that the child could have heard her. The fields weren't fallow yet; it wasn't time to plant the seed.

As they reached the top of the bowl and stared down at the young campers who were still clinging to Adam's energetic monotone, Amy realized that he had assembled her cabinful of girls right in front of him. Had he really expected her to leave? Did he really want her there?

And then, in perfect timing, Amy got the the answer to her question. Adam's eyes lifted to the summit of the bowl as though he'd been glancing toward that very spot all evening, and when he saw her hiking toward him, the grin that swept his own was pure mountain sunshine. The smile she gave him back surged out without permission, a motion that started from somewhere too deep within her to question or restrain.

The last verse of "This Little Light of Mine" petered out and died as Adam stared at her. Belatedly it occurred to Amy that he was waiting for her . . . at least waiting for her to take over the singing. Surely there could be no other reason for the mute radiance that filled his eyes! Suddenly she knew there was no way she could refuse him. God had sent her to Adam

47

Reed as surely as he'd sent her to Camp Colina, and if she ever found the roadway that mapped her return to Christ, it would be through this sage and gentle man.

Carefully she touched Tiffany's shoulder, edging her down the dirt-carved steps to the log where the rest of her cabinmates sat. "Try to get them singing, Tiffany," she urged the child as though they were the best of friends. "The younger kids will follow whatever you do."

Taking the bait, Tiffany straightened just a hair, failing to remember that most of the kids in the camp were just about her age. Her perpetual frown softened with a hint of anticipation. The new look on her face could hardly be called a heart-warming smile, but still, it was a start in that direction.

Amy spared a moment for a self-satisfied grin before she crossed the front of the bowl to Adam's side. *Adam's side.* The words played back in meter. *Took a rib from Adam's side. To make Miss Eve to be his bride.* . . . Suddenly the phrase triggered a memory in her mind, half Biblical, half song. One of her childhood favorites had been a sixteen-verse foot-stomping, hand-clapping southern camp spiritual that told the story of Adam and Eve in the Garden of Eden. It had a rousing chorus that was easy to repeat and used hand motions so she didn't need the guitar. Amy hadn't even thought of the song for years, but suddenly it was imperative that two hundred strangers sing it with her this very instant.

They did. They hooped and hollered, stood and clapped, laughed at the new verse and memorized the chorus. Even Adam's "joyful noise" took on new life when he had a strong singer to follow. By the time the song was over, counselors and campers alike were winded and exuberant. Even Tiffany's blue eyes were sparkling. The stage was set for Adam's informal sermon, sort of a keynote address for the week at Camp Colina.

Amy sat down in the front row only because the girls from Timber Wolf cabin were already there. *I'll find you a pew, Miss Shelby*, he'd promised her. And he'd delivered. But he hadn't promised her she'd feel this good after leading a single song! He hadn't promised her she'd listen so attentively to the first sermon she'd heard in years, or that she'd be so moved by his simple, down home style. She wondered what he did for a living and how he managed to have the summer off to spend at Colina. He was probably a teacher—it was obvious that he had a way with kids and experience speaking before a group. His preaching was so natural that it would have seemed as out of place in a big cathedral as blue jeans at a formal wedding, yet here in the bowl Amy doubted that an ordained minister could have done any better.

He didn't tell them where they'd hike or what they'd make during arts and crafts and how long they had to nap every afternoon. That would come in the morning. What he told them was what he prayed would happen during this magical week in the Sierra. How he wanted each tiny camper to be lifted up a little bit closer to the Lord, and to help each grownup counselor reach a little higher as well. He spoke of the camp family nestled in the hand of the Father, and ended by asking everyone to hold hands in a giant circle as they sang a closing prayer. He didn't even look at Amy before he bowed his head, yet she knew what he expected of her without a single word.

Half an hour ago she could have finished the night with the "Amen" chorus from *Lilies of the Field*, an energetic follow up to her other southern spiritual. Now the tone was ripe for "Dona Nobis Pacem," a delicate round that asked the Lord for peace in every heart and every land. She was afraid the kids wouldn't know it, but it had to be sung anyway.

Amy started it as a solo, high and sweet and pure, and to her surprise Pinky Ferris picked up the second part and two women she didn't know joined in right behind her. A few of the other counselors joined in as they could until they had a full-bodied round echoing in the warm silence of the bowl, their voices whispering through the mountains like a miniature a capella choir. By the time Adam started the benediction—his eyes seeking hers for just a moment before he began to pray—Amy was positively glowing. It was as though she'd never left the grace of Camp Colina.

When the other counselors began to usher their groups back across the meadow, Amy motioned the Timber Wolf campers to follow. Then she stood very quietly as Adam approached her, his eyes dark and warm in the nearby firelight. He didn't speak at first; he just took both her hands and squeezed them gently, then stood perfectly still while he watched her face.

His touch was powerfully reassuring, but it seemed to Amy that his relief was out of proportion to his need to have someone take over Timber Wolf Cabin. Then again, he *did* realize that staying at the camp was essential for her spiritual renewal; he had told her so. And yet—maybe it was just her own need to see such eagerness in his eyes—it seemed to Amy that his pleasure was very personal indeed.

"I still don't have any clothes," she whispered, suddenly awed by the intensity of his gaze. "I don't have any idea what I'm supposed to do."

Abruptly he released her hands, looking unexpectedly sober. "Just follow the path, Amos. Pillsie will bring some things up to your cabin in a few minutes."

She nodded, deciding not to press him.

"Tomorrow you can go into town and get whatever else you really need. Somebody has to go get some supplies after lunch, so you can hitch a ride if you'd rather not go alone."

Again she nodded. "Will I . . . have to lead a Bible study group in the morning?"

Adam pondered her question for a moment before

he answered, "No. If you're really too uncomfortable, Amy, I can fill in for you. But I really think it would be better all the way around if you did it yourself."

"Is there . . . some way I could do it without . . . actually reading from a Bible? You know I'm familiar with Scripture—"

"No problem," he assured her. "The whole program is neatly laid out in a packet of student texts, lovely pictures, and a teacher's guide. The week's theme is 'Parables for the Twentieth Century,' and frankly, I think it does a great job of teaching kids that the stories of Christ are as vital today as they were two thousand years ago."

Amy chuckled. "What a salesman! Did you write this program or do you just draw a commission?"

He shook his head. "Neither. I didn't even pick it out—Orville ordered it last year." His gaze grew solemn. "What do you say, Amy?"

Amy studied his face in the firelight—so handsome, so sensitive, so full of that nameless desire that her presence seemed to kindle within him. She could see that he believed in her. She didn't know why; she wasn't even sure that she believed in herself. But his faith gave her the strength to answer, "I'll do it, Adam. But . . . I'd appreciate if if you'd . . . pray for me."

He grinned. "It's already on the top of list of things to do, Amy."

That seemed to end the discussion. Amy couldn't think of a single intelligent reply, and besides, she knew the girls were waiting. She managed to return Adam's smile, then forced out a hushed, "Goodnight."

He didn't reply right away. Nor did his blue eyes release her own as his steady gaze kept possession of her face. Instead he asked her, "That song . . . about Adam's rib . . . I've never heard it before."

51

Amy was surprised. "It's the most popular song at Camp Colina and not an easy one to forget. When was the last time you were up here?"

He smiled but shook his head. "I've never been up here before. I'd never even heard of this place until I inherited this assignment by surprise in the middle of May."

This time it was Amy who was thunderstruck. He really did need her help! Yet outwardly he was so calm, so self-assured!

"Adam . . . you must have a lot of experience at this sort of thing."

"Sure. I went to camp in Iowa two or three times as a kid." He grinned.

"How can you . . . how can you possibly be prepared to take over here?"

This time he didn't smile. His voice was very quiet as he said simply, "If the Lord didn't think I could handle this, he would have sent me somewhere else this summer." He didn't need to add, *If he didn't think you were ready for this He wouldn't have brought you back here either, Amy!*

Amy didn't answer. She said "Goodnight" again and started up the trail to Timber Wolf Cabin.

"Amos!" His voice stopped her in midstride. "You don't . . . happen to recall where the creation story is, do you? I'd like to check that song against Scripture for accuracy."

He was grinning when she turned back to face him, delighted to be pulling her leg and tossing out another Biblical challenge at the same time.

"Genesis," she told him smugly. "In one of the first few chapters. You've got a Bible. You look it up."

"May I quote you? I mean, may I remind others that . . . a Bible in the hand is worth two or three half forgotten Scriptures chasing through one's mind?"

He looked so happy she couldn't even try to feign

52

anger. For the third time she told him, "*Goodnight, Adam.*"

"Goodnight, Eve."

For just a second Amy was taken aback, but the laughter in his voice caught her in time. A coyote howled in the distance as she briskly waved and turned back to her group. Most of the girls were already ahead of her, chattering in delight. Tiffany showed no interest in the conversation, but kept her flashlight on the path to map out the trail for the other girls.

"Amy!" a familiar small boy's voice reached her as she arrived at Timber Wolf Cabin. "You didn't say goodnight or nothing!"

Amy turned and waited while Joey scampered across the small patch of meadow and threw himself around her knees. With sudden disregard for his fledgling pride and her own juggling act of feelings, she knelt down and hugged him as hard as she could. "Goodnight, little brother," she told him. "You sleep well and do what the Giraffe tells you, but don't forget that if you need me for anything, I'll be right next door."

Joey hugged her back, oblivious to the group of girls skipping past him into the cabin, then kissed her on the cheek before he scurried off to Grizzly. Feeling better than she had in a very long time, Amy closed the door to her own cabin and began supervising the bedtime antics of her ten little ladies.

In the middle of the chaos, Pillsie showed up with a sleeping bag and a plastic sack full of donated and borrowed clothes and sundries. It had been so long since Amy had last spoken to the nurse—not to mention that she'd been a gangly teenager the last time she was at camp—that she didn't expect the older woman to recognize her. She was wrong.

"Nice to see you back here after all this time, Amy," was Pillsie's kindly greeting. Apparently her gruff exterior was reserved for flighty children. "With Orville and Irene gone, we need all the seasoned pros up here we can get."

Honored to be placed in the same class as Grand Slam and Pinky Ferris, Amy asked, "How many of the counselors have been here before, Pillsie?"

"Well—I'd say no more than five or six, just off hand. Cook's new, lifeguard's new, maintenance man hasn't been here more than a month or two—"

"And Adam?" she couldn't help but ask.

A smile touched Pillsie's face. "Somehow I'm not too worried about him. The Lord knew we needed somebody to pull all this together, and by golly, He sent us Adam. That young man is something very special, it seems to me."

It was a long speech of praise for old Pillsie, and Amy was forced to agree. "He does seem to have a . . . unique way of greeting life."

The nurse laughed. "He'll make it all come together. But he is a bit nervous about this first week, so we'll all have to help him out as much as we can, okay?"

Amy nodded. "Thanks for the clothes."

Pillsie shrugged. "No problem. I keep extras of all sizes for assorted emergencies. And you wouldn't believe all the things people leave up here." She walked a few paces toward the lodge before she stopped to add, "By the way, Adam said to tell you that if you need him for anything at all tonight, you just whistle and he'll come running."

Touched by the promise, Amy murmured, "Thank you, Pillsie."

Before she could close the cabin door the other woman tacked on, "That goes for me, too, honey." Amy's eyes met hers for just a moment before the nurse whispered, "I sure was sorry to hear about your mother. I waited every year just to hear her play that old piano."

Again Amy nodded, grateful that she didn't have to speak. Quickly she closed the door and joined the girls, most of whom were already in bed and half asleep. She made the rounds anyway, kissing foreheads, zipping up sleeping bags and discreetly moving teddy bears closer to each tiny pair of arms. For all their eagerness, Amy knew that these children were very young and most of them had never been away from home before. On top of that they'd had to change counselors in midstream, and Amy hadn't had time for more than the most cursory meeting before they'd headed for bed. A little nighttime reassurance was the least she could offer.

She wouldn't have minded some reassurance herself. But none was forthcoming—although both Pillsie and Adam had already offered her more than her fair share—so Amy tugged a flannel nightgown out of her goodwill bag and prepared to climb up onto her bunk.

As she unrolled the freshly cleaned goose down bag it occurred to Amy that she didn't have anything to read. A compulsive bookworm, she could think of no worse fate than facing sleep in a strange bed without a book in her hands! Funny that Adam hadn't known that about her. He'd thought of everything else. . . .

And then she found it, tucked deep within the folds of the zippered bag. Black, with red-lined pages; engraved with gold letters that spelled out clearly that she held in her hands the most sacred property of Adam Christopher Reed.

An hour later she was still holding the Bible, cherished but unopened, when she finally fell asleep.

CHAPTER 4

AMY WOKE UP VERY EARLY the next day. She had always been an early riser, and for the last several years had started each day with a run or a workout. Glancing at her watch and the rows of sleeping heads, she knew she had a good hour before the first bell called the kids to morning watch. What she'd do for a quiet solitary hike above the cabins! But she didn't want to leave the girls alone so early in the game with her own credibility unproven.

The solution arrived as soon as she slipped into her borrowed jeans and sweat shirt and poked her head out the door. Her nearest neighbor to the left was Grand Slam Ferris, who just happened to be sitting on the front porch of Cottontail Cabin reading his Bible. He greeted Amy with a smile and turned back to face the meadow. Quickly she darted over to him, hating to break his solitary meditation.

"Excuse me," she whispered, not wanting even the sound of her voice to intrude on the mystery of the morning, "Will you be here for a while?"

He chuckled. "Are you kidding? It'll take me an

hour just to wake up." His eyes narrowed perceptively. "The pines are calling you north, huh?"

She grinned, unable to deny it.

"Go ahead. I'll keep an eye on your group."

Amy thanked him profusely and skipped up the trail. *Just follow the path, Amos,* Adam had told her. She would do just that! It was a positively glorious day. Hints of sunshine were already brushing the hills; pine needles scented the crisp morning air. There was no wind, no moisture. Nothing to intrude on this exquisite world that God had created just for her.

And for Adam. She felt like a startled deer when she first spotted him hiking toward her, obviously returning from an earlier outing. He did move quietly, like a hunting Sioux, but she was sure it was her own private mood of meditation that had shut out her awareness or another person walking so nearby.

"Good morning, Amos," he greeted her with radiant cheer, two dimples tugging on his smile. He was wearing a bright blue jacket that matched his eyes and a somewhat spiffier pair of jeans than the ones he'd had on yesterday. "I didn't figure you for an early riser."

"You figured wrong, Summit," she retorted playfully, suddenly eager to keep things light and happy between them. Why did just the sight of him seem to take away her wind? "I usually knock out five miles before breakfast."

He grinned. "I might have guessed you were a runner."

She knew he meant well, but the accuracy of his unintentional perception slid right under her defenses and rolled to a stop next to her old tapes. "We can't always face everything with courage, Adam. Even you must have some mossy wounds that you—" She stopped as she saw the darkness drape his face. This incredibly sunny man had hidden wounds!

Amy was stunned by her discovery, and appalled

57

by her bluntness. "Oh Adam," she begged him, "I didn't mean anything by that. I just had a pretty traumatic evening yesterday. I felt so haunted, so uncomfortable. But I'm really trying to stop running now. I think . . . I think maybe I'm really supposed to be here this week. I think it's time for me to make my stand and . . . face these things that still hurt me."

He continued to look at the ground for a moment, then met her eyes and told her stiffly, "I'm sorry if I've contributed to your discomfort, Amy. But I can assure you that my motivation has stemmed solely from my desire to help all my charges at Camp Colina grow."

Amy felt awkward as she studied him. She'd never heard Adam sound so formal and distant. "Am I one of your charges? I mean, now that I've decided to stay?"

He looked surprised. "Of course. Any battered soul is one of my charges. I started praying for you as soon as I realized you were hurting. It had nothing to do with your decision to stay."

It seemed like an odd sort of answer. She knew there were Christians like this . . . who felt that the whole world deserved their tears and compassion . . . but she'd deliberately avoided them for the last few years. Yet now she was both comforted and embarrassed by Adam's inescapable sincerity.

"I was hoping you'd be able to read the Word," he said simply, falling into step with her as they retraced his path up the trail. She didn't question how he knew she hadn't yet opened the Bible; it was just the sort of thing Adam would know. "I really think it would give you comfort right now."

She shook her head, plucking off a clump of pine needles to twist in her hands. "I . . . I'm not ready for that yet, Adam. I still feel. . . ."

"Yes?"

"Well . . . unclean, somehow. I don't think I deserve that . . . relief."

58

Adam stopped as they reached a tiny clearing and lifted both hands to her face. It was a terribly intimate gesture that pierced her soul and forced her to face him . . . and to face herself. He would not let her look away.

"Amy," he whispered, even though they were at least a mile from the nearest human. "Whatever you've done . . . whatever you think you've done . . . God has forgiven you long ago. It's Amy who needs to do the forgiving now."

She tried to stop the tears that snuck by her tightly pressed lids. She failed. "You don't . . . ," she breathed almost brokenly, "You don't know what I did."

"It doesn't matter, Amy." The fingertips that brushed her cheeks felt like tiny angel's wings. "It doesn't matter to me and it surely doesn't matter to God. You've let guilt grab you by the throat . . . ," his hands caressed the delicate skin as if to exorcise the anguish there, " . . . and you've got to break free of it before you can get on with the healing."

He pulled her against his chest, ever so gently, and for just a moment Amy basked in the comfort she found there. But the memory of his reference to her as a "battered soul" forced her to fight the realization that Adam's embrace filled her with a warmth that was much more than comfort, much more than relief. It shouldn't really have surprised her; the ocean waves of longing had been rising and falling between them since she'd first set foot on Camp Colina soil. Yet now, in the silence of the Lord's glorious new morning, she wasn't at all sure that the kind of touch she sought was really the kind that Adam had intended to offer.

Her hesitation communicated itself to Adam. After an awkward moment he let her go, his eyes dark and troubled as she wiped away her remnant tears.

"I know you're not ready to trust me yet," he told

59

her, his voice strangely tense as he ran a nervous hand through his short, sandy hair, "but I don't think you'll ever let it go until you tell *somebody*. Maybe your father, your minister back home, your—"

"Do you mind if we talk about something else?" Amy interrupted, knowing this was not the time to sort out her grief. At the moment she was entirely too puzzled by the conflicting messages she was getting from Adam Reed.

"Of course." He turned back down the trail, gesturing with one hand as though he'd just opened a door for her. "We really ought to be getting back."

Amy fell into step beside him, suddenly feeling almost shy. "Is there . . . anything else I should know about my duties today?"

He nodded. "Yes, as a matter of fact. I'd like you to play the guitar for morning watch if you would. We need to start with a regular opening number—some kind of 'get up out of bed and praise the Lord' type of song—and then we need to end with something they can sing on their way to breakfast every day. I'd also like a background song or two for meditation. Morning watch is more . . . well, it's largely a time of personal prayer."

Amy graced him with a smile. "I know. This isn't my first time here, you may recall."

Adam laughed. "I just don't want to leave anything out. I'm the neophyte, you know! Maybe we should put you in charge of the camp instead. Or we could share the load as partners."

She shook her head. "Just let me get my feet wet this time around, Adam. Let's see how it goes."

"Okay, Amos." The grin on his face reminded her of the first time she'd ever seen him, long and tall in blue jeans, clipboard at the ready. All the magic, the hope, the undeniable appreciation of the woman before him glistened in his eyes once more as they reached the meadow. He held out one hand. "If we can't be partners, Amy, do you think it would be safe to call us friends?''

As Amy slid her small hand into his large one, the magic of his touch warmed her from head to toe. Her smile could not begin to hide her response to the man before her. *Nothing's safe between us, Adam Reed*, she could have told him. Instead she whispered, "Friends, Adam. It's not a bad place to start.''

"You certainly don't waste much time,'' Trevor announced laconically from his perch on the front steps of Grizzly Cabin as Amy waved goodbye to Adam. He was wearing a spotless pale blue shirt and matching corduroy pants that would be destroyed by camp dust within the hour. His dark hair was combed into stylish perfection. "The rest of us are still nestled in our sleeping bags and you and the boss have already staged your first dawn rendezvous.''

He was smiling, more or less, so Amy decided to pretend he was only teasing. "It's a beautiful morning, isn't it, Trevor?'' she greeted him airily, determined not to take offense. "I can't get over how clear the air is up here.''

Trevor crossed his arms and studied her face. "I take it you're resigned to staying here for a while?''

Her smile was a bit more forced this time. "Yes, as a matter of fact. I'm rather looking forward to the week.''

"I'll bet you are.''

This time there was no mistaking his intent. Amy stopped before she reached her own steps and faced him squarely. "I'm bearing a cross or two of my own here, Trevor. I'm not asking you to help me carry the load but you don't need to stick out your foot and trip me as I pass by, either.''

Genuine surprise washed across his face as Amy reached her cabin. It was mirrored by the young girl who stood in the doorway as Amy marched inside. In

61

sharp contrast to her father's dapper attire, Tiffany wore faded blue jeans and a colorless gray sweatshirt that looked like a refugee from the rag pile. For just a second she looked abashed by Amy's welcoming smile, then demanded, "Where have you been? Aren't you supposed to be taking care of us?" She sounded for all the world like an irate parent waiting for a teenager who's just broken curfew, but she looked like a little girl who'd woken up in the night afraid of the dark.

"I've been for a walk, Tiffany. I asked the man next door to keep an eye on you."

"You mean my *father?*" The word dripped with disgust. "He's keeping an eye on me anyway. He's been acting like a spy ever since we got here."

Amy sighed. Last night's progress with Tiffany must have been a mirage. She still had a long, long way to go with this child; she'd have to try another approach. "Is anybody else up yet?" she asked, determined not to start the day in a parental tug-of-war.

"How would I know?" Tiffany countered belligerently. "D'you think I care what they do?"

For a moment Amy was actually speechless. Then, making a conscious decision, she forced herself to say, "Yes, as a matter of fact, I think you care a great deal. And I think you'll be very sorry if you go out of your way to be as nasty to them as you've been to me. I'm likely to give you another chance because I'm an adult. Most seven-year-olds aren't nearly so forgiving. They don't want anything to do with somebody who acts like a spoiled baby."

Amy left Tiffany with her mouth hanging open as she marched back into the main part of the cabin. She wasn't really an advocate of shock treatment, but the 'gentle and loving' approach certainly wasn't getting her anywhere with this child. And one thing was certain: before this week was out, she *would* have

Tiffany Grant turned around and on the road toward a normal, happy childhood. No matter what it took.

She crept silently over to her sleeping bag on the top bunk and straightened it up, then glanced in her grab bag of goodies to see what, if anything, she could choose from in the way of morning sundries. Somehow she tipped the bag too far, and a tube of toothpaste slid out onto the floor. As she leaned down to pick it up, a small hand lifted it from the ground and thrust it toward her.

Amy bent down to see her benefactor, a small, curly-haired child with a shy grin and sleep in her eyes.

"I'm sorry, Julie Ann," Amy whispered, hoping she'd remembered the right name after last night's brief greetings. "Did I wake you up?"

Julie Ann shook her dark head, broadening her pixie smile. "No. I was already awake." She rubbed her eyes and tried to sit up. "What are we going to do today?"

"Well, first of all we're going to go to morning watch. Do you know what that is?"

Julie Ann shook her head.

"Well, it's sort of like going to church, only it's going to be outside in the meadow. We're all going to sing a little and pray a little. Okay?"

Amy was greeted by a nod, then the question, "What comes after that?"

She eased herself beneath the top bunk to sit next to the little girl. As she started to speak, she realized that Tiffany had trailed her into the room and now stood by the door, doing her best to look bored and disinterested as she listened to every word.

"Well, after that comes breakfast. Then you'll go to your Bible study group—"

"With you?"

"Well . . . ," Amy studied the anxious young face, "I don't know, Julie Ann. I'll have a group, but I don't know if you'll be in it. When I came here as a little girl we were all mixed up for the Bible groups so we got to know all the other kids and counselors in the camp, but there was always at least one other girl from my cabin in the group. I'm sure there will be somebody there you know."

Julie Ann bit her lip apprehensively. "So after the Bible group, do I get to see you again?"

After Tiffany's acerbic greeting, it was heartwarming to find a child who was so eager for Amy's company! She grinned at the little girl and promised, "You bet. We'll be given some kind of work detail— cleaning the lodge or fixing up the bowl or part of the trail—and then we go to lunch."

Before she could explain the rest of the day—which would have been a product of her hazy memory rather than an accurate description of Adam Reed's new Camp Colina—the first bell began to ring with such volume and energy that Amy was positive that Adam was the one on the bell pull.

"Rise and shine, girls!" she declared cheerfully to her crew of surprised and moaning sleepers. "Fifteen minutes till morning watch. Just hustle on out any way you can. We'll come back and clean up the cabin later."

Careful not to bang her head on the upper bunk as she stood up, Amy began to tour the room, shaking young shoulders as she started each girl's day off with a smile. It was not until she had the whole group rounded up at the door that she realized that Tiffany, who had been fully dressed even before the first bell, had returned to her bunk and was now simulating sleep, her face against the wall.

Amy decided to ignore her for the time being, hoping she'd join the other girls if they all feigned disinterest. Besides, she had enough to do. By the time she retrieved her guitar from the car and tuned it up, eighty or ninety little people were gathered in the sun-grazed meadow waiting for Adam's first breath of dawn prayer. Amy perched on a massive rock that served as a natural altar and begin to sing, "Rise, Shine, Give God the Glory, Glory," encouraging the children to join her. Most of them knew the song and those who didn't chimed in anyway. By the time she'd finished the last verse almost every child in the camp was ready for worship. Tiffany had edged out of the cabin and now sat on the front steps glaring at her father and the assembled worshipers in defiant isolation.

But Trevor didn't seem to see her. His eyes were on Joey, who was bouncing up and down with such enthusiasm that anyone over the age of seventeen would have grown tired just watching him!

Amy managed an indulgent smile at her exuberant little brother before she laid a single finger against her lips in a none-too-subtle hint for him to follow Trevor's orders.

When Joey and the others began to settle down, Grand Slam read the Seventeenth Psalm, then another counselor whose name Amy could not recall shared a true story about how prayer had changed her life. Amy didn't know when Adam had arranged for these staff contributions, but he'd obviously done his homework. One of the things she'd always loved most about Camp Colina was that it thrived because *everybody* participated. Most weeks during the summer there was at least one minister at the camp, but the lay leadership was so vigorous and sincere that a professional clergyman was a luxury rather than a necessity.

With a single glance in Amy's direction after the other woman's testimony, Adam invited her to sing. In quiet, prayerful tones she hummed a popular morning worship song, singing alternate verses as the spirit moved her. The meadow grew very still and golden as she sang, and when she finished, Adam bowed his head and asked the Lord to bless each precious soul around him. Amy waited for several minutes before she started "Lord, I want to Be a Christian" in muted, a capella tones; then she picked up both her guitar and the tempo, leading the worshipers to breakfast in a sunburst of joyful song.

When they reached the lodge, Pinky Ferris—her face crowned with sparkling blue eyes and the Lord's own loving smile—came up to Amy and whispered, "Your music is truly blessed, Amos. You and Adam work together like you've been planning services as a team for years. I'm so glad the Lord sent you to us this week."

Amy was so surprised she could hardly smile, but she did manage a heartfelt thank you before she found her way to the place Julie Ann had saved for her. The little girl's brown eyes glistened with excitement. "I just love the way you sing. I really like that song about the 'kangaroosies that came in by twosies.'"

Amy laughed. "That was always one of my favorites, too."

She couldn't help but wonder what Tiffany had thought of the song, alone on the steps of Timber Wolf Cabin. She had taken her breakfast to a distant table and was eating there in deliberate, remote silence with only the yellow jackets for company. Amy really didn't know quite what to try next with the girl; she was rapidly running out of options. She was tempted to talk to Trevor about his daughter, but it was already obvious that he didn't know what to do with her either. Adam was a better choice, but Amy wanted to hold on to him as a court of last resort. She suspected that once she brought in the big guns with Tiffany, she'd be helpless forever after without them.

She was just about to get up when a large, gentle hand settled on her shoulder, sending unplanned chills throughout her body. She didn't need to look up at Adam's face to know whose touch had moved her; no

66

other man could have flustered her so. She didn't know why he had this effect on her. She dated often enough to have her choice of interesting men, and none of them had ever caused such a tailspin of jumbled feelings by the tiniest look or subtle touch! She felt confused and radiant when he was near; she craved his praise and approval and desperately wanted to live up to his expectations.

"I knew it would be perfect," Adam whispered, squeezing her shoulder just once before he walked away.

Amy closed her eyes, admitting, for the first time, that she would be terribly disappointed if it turned out that this man's interest in her was only spiritual. And yet, remembering the look she'd seen in his eyes more than once, she was almost certain that he returned her inexplicably turbulent feelings.

"What did he mean?" Julie Ann asked before Amy had recovered enough to answer.

She stared at the child's eager face, struggling for words that conveyed the truth of Adam's feelings, if not her own. It was hard to explain something that she herself did not yet fully understand. At last she managed to stammer, "Julie Ann . . . I think he meant he liked the song about the 'kangaroosies,' too."

The little girl rewarded Amy with a beatific smile.

There were nine children in the Redwood Room when Amy got there. They sat uncertainly around the oak barrel table, trying to balance their desire to be pious with their impulse to giggle at each cheerful new face.

"Here's the list," one of the boys announced, handing Amy a yellow piece of legal pad paper that had apparently been taped to the door. "Almost everybody's here."

Amy smiled and checked the list, calling off names as she tried to match the new faces. A couple of last minute changes had been made, both of them involving girls from her cabin. She wondered if Adam's insight was responsible for the addition of shy Julie Ann and belligerent Tiffany as Timber Wolf's representatives. The two girls he'd placed elsewhere to accommodate them were both very self-assured young ladies who would have been a great asset to the group . . . and would have felt at home anywhere.

Tiffany, of course, was nowhere to be seen. But Julie Ann, looking nervous and acutely shy, fairly bloomed when Amy sent her a "You're my girl" smile and asked her to lead off the introductions.

"Has anybody been to a church camp before?" Amy asked a few minutes later, trying to get a base from which to work.

Two boys raised their hands.

"I came here last year," one said.

"I went to this place in Texas with my uncle Lou when I was just a kid," declared another with all the wisdom of his not-quite-seven years.

Amy smiled. "Have any of you been to Sunday School or summer Bible school?"

This time everybody's hand went up—even Julie Ann's. She didn't say a word but her eyes sparked with interest as she watched the others.

"Well, gang, my name is Amos, and as you probably know, I have been to church camp before— this one, as a matter of fact—but it's been a long time so you'll have to help me if I forget what I'm supposed to do. Okay?"

"Okay, Amos!" they all agreed cheerfully.

Amy skimmed the teacher's guide for the first story as she passed out the books. As an experienced teacher, she hadn't really expected any difficulty conducting this class. But her hopes collided in unplanned panic when she discovered the topic for the day: the prodigal son.

Why didn't he tell me! she hollered in her heart. *Why didn't he give me a chance to back out!*

Quickly she realized that she was being unfair. Adam *had* offered her an escape hatch, and he couldn't be expected to know how hard this particular parable might hit her, since she still hadn't confided in him. Forcing herself to complete the task assigned— Adam, after all, was counting on her—she smiled at the children and asked for volunteers to read.

Almost everyone raised his hand, and she wished Tiffany had been there to feel the communal enthusiasm. Surely it would have touched the child! But her chair remained empty, and the book before it stayed closed. Inwardly, Amy sighed. She was going to have to surrender this problem to Adam.

She asked one of the boys to read the title under the collection of pictures that represented "prodigals" of several types and found it easy to lead the children into a discussion.

"Does anybody know what a prodigal is?" she asked. Several tried to answer, but at first no one really seemed to know. Then a girl named Marty suggested, "I think it's like . . . some guy who just goes off without telling anybody, and then he gets in trouble."

It wasn't a bad beginning. Amy used the girl's comment to lead into the story. It was written in simple language, but she decided to read it out loud. This was, after all, a Bible lesson, not a second grade reading group!

Somewhere near the last page—when she had to stop to explain the words "fatted calf"—a motion near the door caught Amy's eye. She was sure the drab gray sleeve belonged to Tiffany, but she didn't reveal the slightest hint of interest as she continued reading the story. By the time she was finished, Tiffany had found the empty chair at the table. Hunched and sullen, she said nothing as she gripped her closed book with both hands.

"Look, Amos!" Julie Ann declared in genuine delight. "Tiffany's here!"

Tiffany glared at the other girl, but Amy said evenly, "Yes, Julie Ann. Remember I told you that you'd probably have a friend from our cabin here at Bible study?"

This time the glare was directed at Amy instead of Julie Ann, but Tiffany said nothing as Amy smiled and went on with the lesson.

There were a number of suggested questions in her teacher's guide about the meaning of the parable, and an extended discussion on the meaning of parables themselves. But Amy decided to skip that for the moment and redirect the children to the family pictures at the front on the story.

"Why do you think there's a picture of an Eskimo when the story I just told you took place in Palestine?" she asked the group. She was answered by blank stares. "Why do you think there's a picture of two kids on a beach with their mother?"

"Maybe they're just listening to the story," Jeffrey suggested.

"I think they're waiting for their big brother," Marty offered.

Tiffany said nothing. She studied her book intently, never acknowledging Amy's casual gaze.

"The important thing about these pictures," Amy declared when the children ran out of suggestions, "is that we understand that Jesus wasn't just telling us a story about some people who lived a long time ago and don't matter anymore. Any one of us could be the son who left, the son who stayed, or the father who did the forgiving."

"I can't be a boy!" a girl in pig tails insisted, speaking for the first time. "I can't be a daddy, either."

"Of course not. But don't you think Jesus could have told this story about a mother with two little girls? Wouldn't it have come out the same?"

This stopped the children for just a moment. Then

Jeffrey smiled. "Yeah. Girls do just as many dumb things as boys."

Tiffany tossed him a hostile glance, but still she said nothing.

"It's not just children," Amy insisted, hoping somebody else would say what Tiffany had to hear. "Sometimes it's the grownups who forget their responsibilities and run away for a while. Sometimes a mom or dad will be tired or hurting or confused and make some pretty bad mistakes. When they have enough courage and sense to come back and beg for forgiveness, then it's up to you guys—the kids—to be like the father was in this parable and kill the fatted calf."

Tiffany's scowl intensified, but Amy held her smoldering gaze until the girl backed down. Her next words were still for Tiffany, but now her eyes took in all the children in the room.

"I'm not saying that it's right for parents or kids to do mean things to each other. But love—Christian love—doesn't always have anything to do with right and wrong. It has to do with forgiveness and starting fresh. That's really what this story is all about. That's what Jesus was trying to show us when he told it. That's why it's written down in the Bible—so people can read this story and learn from it again and again and again."

This time the sensation of someone standing in the doorway took Amy by surprise, and she jerked visibly as she met Adam's eyes. He looked so tall, so beautifully virile and casually handsome . . . so spiritually open and so eager to heal her! He nodded just once—ever so slightly—but his wordless praise caused a domino reaction of red blush and glow that Amy was powerless to conceal.

Nervously she glanced at her watch when at left, grateful and surprised to note that she'd run almost five minutes overtime on her first day as a Bible teacher.

Not bad, Amos, she told herself smugly as she told the kids to pile their books in a corner and report to their work stations. *Not bad at all.*

Tiffany was the first one out of the room.

CHAPTER 5

AFTER THE BIBLE CLASS was over, it didn't take Amy long to gather up the Timber Wolf girls and start out on the morning's trail maintenance assignment posted at the lodge. It took even less time for her to regret being paired up with Trevor.

"Nobody told me I'd be on shovel detail my first morning here," he groused when Amy told him they'd been assigned the trail on the way to the chapel. "It looks okay to me. What do they want us to do, anyway?"

Amy was astonished when Tiffany appeared from under her left wing and answered for her. "They want us to clear out the pine needles and smooth out the trail. Sort of like weeding the garden and raking the leaves back home." She turned to Amy, defiance and pain blurring her pretty young features. "I used to help Mama do the yardwork. Nobody else ever did."

Amy suspected that the outburst was intended more to wound her father than to proclaim any particular interest in trail repair, but the vigor in the young voice still surprised her. Trevor said nothing as his daughter picked up a shovel and began to level out the trail, but the look on his face reminded Amy of his brief confession the night before. *No wonder these two are having so much trouble with each other!* she told herself. *They don't have any idea how to ask anyone for help . . . or how to come right out and say they're hurting.* Despite the way they both needled her, Amy couldn't help but wish there was something more she could do for them.

Trevor didn't seem to notice when Amy took over the task of organizing his boys as well as his girls. He made no further comments about the trail or the work assignment. She also noticed that he seemed to have given up on his shirt and pants; the morning's brand-new outfit already looked like his Saturday working-on-the-car clothes, but he didn't seem to lament the loss. Maybe he was learning.

Amy loved working outdoors and had no complaints about maintaining the lower side of the Jordan River. She didn't want to go back inside the chapel, but she was eager to keep the trail open for anyone else who could. She got the children to sing as they worked, and after a while even Trevor joined in. His voice was better than Adam's, and he seemed to have more than a passing acquaintance with the church camp music of Amy's youth. Tiffany continued to sulk, but—to her credit and to Amy's surprise—she worked as hard as any other two campers on the trail. After half an hour's observation of her diligent silence, Amy skirted the trail to her side and tried to make conversation.

"You're really a good worker, Tiff." She tried to mask her surprise. "I take it you really like helping your mom outside."

Tiffany shrugged. "He never helped. He never did anything at all to help her."

Amy swallowed half a dozen retorts, suddenly anxious to know where Tiffany had been living during her separation from Trevor. No child her age would have stopped to consider her mother's welfare with such caustic insight without prodding; clearly it was a phrase she'd heard many times before. Still determined to gain the girl's trust, Amy did not try to defend Trevor but asked instead, "Where is your mother now, Tiffy?"

Looking straight at her, Tiffany replied in a voice as cold as glass, "She's dead."

For several moments Amy could not speak. She knew Tiffany wanted her to be stunned, to protest, to offer words of sympathy that she could reject while the chip on her shoulder multiplied exponentially. Instead Amy told her in her gentlest voice, "I lost my mother, too. It still hurts me sometimes."

Her unexpected honesty leveled Tiffany. Tears suddenly welled in her proud, anguished eyes as she turned away and attacked the trail with a vengeance. Amy wanted to put her arms around her, to rock her till the moment passed, but she knew the youngster still wasn't ready to receive that comfort. But still she was certain that her deepest instincts had been correct. She hadn't coddled the child, but she'd addressed her pain as a peer. She was certain she'd gained a minute toehold on the edge of Tiffany's trust.

"So what's this chapel for, anyway?" Trevor asked somewhat gruffly when Amy was once again within earshot. "We've already got the lodge, the bowl, and the meadow. How many places do people here need to pray?"

Amy scowled at him. Every time she began to think there was some hope for this man, he slid down a notch or two in her esteem. "You can never have too many places to pray, Trevor. For your information, this chapel is the only place in the camp where there's a piano, which provides a very different kind of worship experience than an open meadow." She knew her mother could have explained it more

75

clearly. Amy herself could have made her point more dramatically by dragging him up the hill and making him listen while she tried to commune with the Lord by way of the keyboard. But that was impossible. It was bad enough that Adam had already caught her up there seeking the impossible once. She'd never risk it again.

"When it's raining up here—sometimes in the summer but especially during the winter conferences and seminars held up here—the chapel is used a lot," she continued quietly. "It's a very special place."

Too special to share with you, she heard her heart echo. She knew that Adam, the soul of forgiveness, would chastise her for her lack of tolerance. Trevor had exposed a bit of his heart yesterday; she knew he was hurting. Still, he was doing his best to behave like a boor, and she was getting tired of it.

Abruptly the bell began to clang, followed by the sound of Adam's greeting from the base of the trail. At first his eyes seemed to take in the whole crew, but soon they came to rest on Amy. She couldn't hold back the smile that radiated in answer to his own; she waited in readiness for the words she was certain he would direct just to her. But suddenly his glance took in Trevor, still standing close beside her, and whatever message might have reached her was stilled.

"You're free on parole until tomorrow, kids!" he called up to the group in general. "You've got fifteen minutes to get cleaned up for lunch, so let's hop to it!"

With a chorus of celebration, the kids tossed down their shovels and rakes and bolted for the lodge. Before Amy could recall two or three to help carry the tools, Adam had commandeered several eager volunteers from her cabin to come back and help. Babbling like parakeets, they all but tripped over each other trying to carry the most equipment . . . or perhaps trying to impress the handsome young camp director.

"Amazing, isn't it?" Trevor drawled with a hint of a sneer, his eyes flicking from Adam to Amy and then back to the girls. "He doesn't seem like the type, but the effect that man has on women is incredible. No matter how young or old—"

"It's not amazing at all!" Amy countered, discarding what was left of her patience. "The man exhibits common decency and every day courtesy. That's more than enough to distinguish him from the local competition!"

She could have extended Adam's list of virtues, but she knew she'd made her point as she glared at Trevor. Looking more than a little chagrined, he sucked on his lower lip and muttered, "I'm really not doing very well with you, am I?"

"No," Amy agreed. "You're not." She stifled several other less charitable comments before she managed to say, "But if you'd like to start over again, I'd be willing to forgive and forget."

His face lit up. Suddenly he looked more pitiful than offensive. "Really?"

"Really." *This man is too pathetic to earn my contempt*, she suddenly decided. *He's in a lot worse shape than I am.*

Trevor studied her face for several moments before he declared, "I'm sorry, Amy. I guess I've been pretty obnoxious."

Amy could have agreed with him, but she took mercy on the man and said nothing.

"I guess . . . I guess I haven't been around such a . . . nice Christian girl in some time, Amy, and I feel helpless without my usual lines. I don't know how to play the game this way. In the mountains I'm like a fish out of water anyway, and Tiffany makes me feel like I'm some kind of a leper—"

"It's okay, Trevor. A little apology goes a long way with me."

He smiled, unable to conceal his relief. "I'll try to do better from here on in. Really."

"Glad to hear it. Right now I think we better head for the lodge while there's still something left to eat."

He nodded, then stopped to offer her one hand as Adam had at dawn. "Friends?"

"Friends," she relented, taking his hand for just a moment.

It didn't feel the least bit like Adam's.

"Amy!" Pillsie called over the clamor of lunch. "Adam said the truck's leaving right now if you want to go. I'll keep an eye on your girls till you get back."

"So that's all he wanted to tell me," she muttered to herself, stifling a pang of disappointment. Not really certain how to take the nurse's words—as a generous gesture or a command—Amy returned her empty plate to the pile and trotted down to the parking lot. Since Adam was nowhere in sight, she couldn't ask him who was driving into town or why had hadn't mentioned that she'd have to forfeit lunch to go along. More than a little miffed, she approached the truck uncertainly, considering telling the driver to forget the whole thing. She could eat with the kids and drive herself down later.

The passenger door slid open in anticipation of Amy's arrival. Before she could speak her words were arrested by the smiling blond face before her.

"I'm glad you decided on the corn dogs," was Adam's greeting. His dimples promised her an hour of fun and laughter.

"I beg your pardon?" It was hard to be angry in the face of his high spirits, but she still wasn't sure what he had in mind.

"Every now and then I get this corn dog fetish. It occurred to me that since we were going down anyway, we could sneak in a bit of junk food for lunch. I wasn't sure if Pillsie could convince you to give up a meal on the hill."

"Considering the royal summons she issued on

your behalf, I didn't feel I had much choice." Amy's tone was restrained, but her fleeting anger had already evaporated.

Adam looked more than a bit chagrined. "Oh, Amy, I'm really sorry if it came across that way. I was so sure you'd want to come along that I didn't take the time to issue a proper invitation. I wasn't sure I could ask you on the trail and get away without inviting . . . well, everybody within earshot." He reached across the pickup cab for her hand. "I would be honored, Miss Shelby, by the pleasure of your company for luncheon this fine day at . . . " he glanced at his watch, " . . . precisely twelve thirty o'clock in the afternoon."

Even if the smile on his face hadn't melted her, the warmth of his fingers would have. The most subtle touch from this man seemed to awaken her senses. A simple smile could render her speechless.

"I'd be honored, sir."

He pulled her into the ancient camp truck and started the motor. He looked relieved that it turned over instantly. "I can't believe all the nuts and bolts it takes to run a church camp, Amy. Every day I discover something new we don't have, or something that doesn't seem to work as well as everybody remembers it from last year. I've had to go into town almost every day since I got here."

Considering the pitted and pot-holed trail necessary for that journey, Amy knew he wasn't just making an idle lament. "How long have you been up here, Adam?"

"Two weeks. I was almost starting to feel at home until all the kids showed up."

Amy laughed. "Surely they don't intimidate you! I've never seen a man more comfortable with children."

He shrugged off her praise. "I adore them, Amy. But I have to admit that I've had a lot more experience with teenagers and college kids than these smaller ones. More than that, I think, is the . . . tremendous sense of responsibility I feel for their welfare. They're just so young! And it's not as though I'm with them every minute. I have to trust them to a whole flock of strangers—church folks, I know, but strangers I didn't even get to choose—and it makes me uneasy."

For a moment Amy was silent. The jarring of the truck seemed to fill the air between them before she said, "It may seem to you that I'm standing in spiritual quicksand, Adam, but nobody's ever questioned my trustworthiness with children. I—"

"Amy!" He looked shocked. "I didn't mean you! If I had a daughter in your cabin I wouldn't lose a wink of sleep all night!"

Amy studied him quietly. "Thank you, but I assumed you were referring to me. I'm the only substitute counselor you've got—"

"Amy, I thought I told you last night that I inherited the whole lot of them. Since Orville retired there's been a lot of upheaval in the camp program, with several people—good people—tossing around the hot potato. The lay leader who was scheduled to take over had a heart attack last month, and every minister in the Conference started scrambling for a replacement. The head pastor at my church nominated me—probably because most of my kids disappear in the summer anyway—so here I am."

Amy had a lot of questions to ask about this fascinating man, but she tried not to sound nosy. "Where are you from, anyway?" was her first casual probe. "You're a long way from Iowa."

He laughed. "But still in the farm belt. I live in Davis. College town."

Amy nodded. She knew that the University of California branch located near Sacramento was famous for agricultural education and veterinary medicine. "I've been there a few times. It's a lovely place."

"You bet it is!" His enthusiasm was unforced. "The most wonderful thing about it—aside from the herds of roaming bicycles, the free cultural events on campus and the incredible country air—is that a lot of the small town prejudices I grew up with just seem to be absent there. The students and the farmers live side by side with almost no friction. They just accept each other and smile a lot."

"Sounds like a fair description of the driver of this truck."

Again he laughed, his male baritone warming the air between them. "I'm no saint, Amy, but I have tried to model my life after Jesus'. He made it pretty clear that His love was based on forgiveness, not judgment and reprimand." He shot her a meaningful look. "You'd do well to remember that."

It was an opening to discuss her past, but Amy didn't take it. She just wasn't in the mood for self-reflection. It was a beautiful day; she was sitting next to the most exciting man she'd ever met in her life, surrounded by the most exquisite view in all the Sierra Madre range. She wasn't going to spoil it with past griefs.

"Isn't that Persistence Peak?" she asked, pointing to the towering mountain—Camp Colina's crowning glory—that was still visible as they approached the town.

"Yes, ma'am. I've driven up pretty close to the summit on the dirt road—trail, actually—to Orville and Irene's, but I haven't hiked up our side to the top. I hear that the view is spectacular."

"Oh, it is! We made the climb every year. It seemed so far when I was little, but getting there was such a triumph!"

He grinned. "I wonder if your counselors saw it that way."

She had to laugh. "I never asked them. But every time I hiked up with my parents, my dad kept us all in stitches most of the time, and whenever he stopped making jokes my mother got us singing. So I really never noticed I was tired until it was all over."

"Sounds like a trip to Disneyland."

"I guess it was, in a way. But there was always a sense of . . . well, spiritual completion, I guess, when we finally reached the top. No matter how much fun we had at camp, we didn't really feel ready to go home until we'd made the hike to Persistence Peak."

This time his gaze was pensive. "I take it that a hike is on the agenda for Timber Wolf Cabin this week?"

Surprised by the depth of her resistance to the idea, Amy looked away. "I don't know, Adam. Maybe nobody else will want to go."

"That doesn't have a thing to do with it, Amy. If it's part of the process of healing you need—"

"You said your nickname was Summit," she interrupted, deliberately trying to sidetrack him. "Is that in honor of some other mountain?"

For just a moment Adam sobered, then told her simply, "Not really."

"Not really what? It's not your nickname or they don't call you that because of a mountain?"

At first she didn't think he was going to answer, and his hesitation made Amy wish she could recall the question. It had seemed like a harmless enough inquiry! But his face seemed to darken a bit as he told her, "Formal titles—even Mr. and Mrs.—just don't seem right at camp, but a lot of the kids and parents are uncomfortable with first names for adults. So everybody seems to come with a nickname or gets stuck with one here." He sighed. "Summit is the only nickname I've ever had, so I thought I'd toss it out before I got saddled with something even worse."

"So far, so good," Amy prodded, reluctant to press

82

him but growing increasingly curious about his past. "But you still haven't answered the question."

He glanced at Amy with unveilable sadness before he gave in; his reluctance made her regret her insistence. "A friend of mine used to call me 'Summit' whenever she was particularly aggravated with me. After hearing it for the last twenty-four hours I've remembered that I never cared for it much. I guess I should have let somebody up here make one up."

Without knowing why, Amy suddenly felt sorry for him. It was the second time today that this sunny man had revealed one of his ancient wounds to her, and she wondered how many more he might be hiding. "Adam," she told him gently, "if I were the one talking and you were the one listening, I know you'd tell me to get it off my chest."

He smiled—still a bit sadly—as he parked under a sign that proudly proclaimed they'd just arrived at Jimmy's World Famous Corn Dogs and Other Great Stuff. He turned off the motor and reached for the door, then stopped and turned to Amy.

"Okay. I'll make it brief . . . and off the record, Amy."

Her eyes promised him the confidentiality he sought.

"I had a geometry class in college. I was absolutely lousy at math, and I can't imagine what I was doing in there to begin with. But one day we got an assignment—extra credit, extra challenge, something like that—which had to do with some rock climber winding his way to the summit of a mountain. I forget the details, but I remember working and reworking that problem till I was purple. Every day I'd show up with some new bizarre answer, and every day the prof would applaud my determination but tell me I was wrong. After a week, everybody else had given up altogether and asked him to just give us the answer."

He glanced at his keys, as though they held some

83

ancient mystery. "Linda was really the brain in the class, and everybody figured that if *she* couldn't figure it out, poor old Adam Reed—a history major, no less—surely didn't stand a chance. They all really pressed the prof to tell us the answer, and Linda got pretty uppity about it. But he was determined to let me keep struggling—said I had a 'summit' of my own to reach."

He smiled at her in a moment's chagrin. "I've always been that way about school. About everything, I guess. All or nothing. If I do it at all, I do it till it's perfect. I don't cut any corners. I don't lie to myself. I just—"

He was watching her so intently that he suddenly forgot his story. His eyes had that same look she remembered from the first moment they'd met—as though he were looking deep inside her, reading her heart, reading her mind. *Does he know that I want him?* she asked herself, suddenly shocked to admit the depth of her longing even to herself. *Does he know that I'm more drawn to him than I've ever been to any man in my life?*

"Are you hungry?" he asked abruptly, seeming to discard his tale. "I've tasted better corn dogs at the Sacramento State Fair, but these will do."

Amy smiled. "Yes, I'm hungry, but finish your story first. *Did* you ever solve your problem?"

He stared at her with sudden anguish that he could not hide. Was she the cause of his pain? Or did it stem from some lingering memory that still haunted him from time to time?

"Yes," he finished with his customary cheer, wiping the memory from his eyes. "I solved the problem. The professor was elated, the class was humbled, and Linda fell at my feet like a sack of potatoes. She was awed by my brilliance and determination, which she applauded ever after by calling me 'Summit' whenever she thought I was being unnecessarily stubborn in pursuit of some lofty goal that struck her as utterly pointless." His smile was almost genuine. "And that's the whole story, Amos. Are you sure you like corn dogs?"

"I'm sure," she insisted as she helped her from the truck. She was also sure that she'd only heard the least important part of Adam's tale. It was riddled with holes, and every tear in the fabric of his memory seemed to be embroidered with thread that spelled a single feminine word: *Linda*.

Quite suddenly, Amy took an acute dislike to the name.

From the moment Adam ushered her into the drive-in, she felt like they'd just started on their first date. He insistent on paying for lunch, going for the food, gathering napkins and straws and packets of catsup and mustard.

"So tell me about your job. Kay said you teach music, but that's about it."

"I teach band at Bayview High, and also chorus and a string orchestra. But I have to admit that the fall marching band is my single badge of glory. My kids are *terrific!*"

Adam looked impressed. "I always thought marching band leaders were men."

"They usually are—just because they're more likely to have backgrounds in brass and percussion. But when I was in fourth grade and ready to join the band—dying to play the clarinet—my father took out his old trombone and said, 'See this trombone, Amy? We've already paid for this trombone. We don't have to rent this trombone. We have a carrying case for this trombone. Therefore you will—'"

"I get it. Were you disappointed?"

"Actually, I thought it was kind of fun to be the only girl in the section. But my arms were to short to play seventh position . . . ," she demonstrated the longest stretch of a slide trombone, " . . . and when I got braces, I went back to the piano full time."

Adam laughed. "Braces! I bet that hurt."

"You're not kidding. These days when parents ask me to recommend an instrument for their children, the first thing I do is look at their teeth!"

Still chuckling, Adam studied her mouth and declared, "I'm glad the trombone lost. You've got a beautiful smile." Her smile widened as he continued. "Actually, I got the impression that you taught music to little kids."

"I do. At a private music store after school."

He shook his head. "You're really quite gifted, Amy. Some church choir must be crying out for a person like you."

Abruptly the smile slid off her face. "I can't sing in a choir, Adam. I can't even go to church. I've tried half a dozen times—in half a dozen different places. I've always left in tears. One time the minister was worried enough to find out who I was and come to see me. He was very kind, but I just . . . I was too embarrassed to tell him anything."

For a moment Adam was silent. Then he suggested, "Maybe the minister you grew up with would be your best bet. Is he still at your . . . father's church?"

Amy shook her head. "He left about the time I went to college. I'm not even sure where he is."

"I'm sure you could find him. *I* could find him. And if he's like most of the pastors I've known, he would be more than—"

"Don't. Please." Her eyes begged him to drop the subject. "You're pushing me too hard, Adam."

He backed off, but his eyes could not conceal his impatience. She knew he wanted to heal her—prescribe an antibiotic and get her over the flu—but it wasn't that easy. As much as she admired him, she was beginning to resent his insistence.

They finished eating in silence and ordered hot

fudge sundaes for dessert. After a while the conversation moved on to other things. California and the midwest; life on a farm and life in the city; brothers and sisters and growing up alone.

"I miss them sometimes," Adam confessed after telling Amy about his large farm family and the happy times that had colored his childhood. "I usually go home for Christmas, but other than that I don't see them very often. I've got a brother that made it as far west as Idaho, and he drives down to see me every now and again." He paused, remembering these visits with evident joy. "It's such a relief being with somebody who's known me since I was a kid. Somebody who sees past my position and just treats me like . . . well, like anybody else."

"You're so lucky! I always wanted a brother," Amy told him sincerely, forgetting about Joey for the moment. Something about his plea to be treated like "anybody else," scratched at her curiosity, but before she could follow through on that perception Adam began to speak.

"Every family's different, Amy. I've seen some where one child was way too many and others where ten weren't nearly enough. As long as it works—that's what matters."

Her thoughts swept briskly to Tiffany. Had the youngster's family setting ever worked? Sooner or later Amy knew she'd have to discuss Tiffany with Adam, but she decided that this wasn't the time. A few signs of progress were already evident, and Amy very much wanted to solve at least one of her problems without resorting to Adam's help. She also didn't want anything to intrude on their brief time together.

"In my case my parents wanted more children, Adam, but for some medical reason that nobody ever really figured out, I was their only baby." She smiled at the memory. "Mother always called me 'her little miracle.' "

Very gently Adam said, "I take it she's gone now."

Amy nodded, not really wanting to talk about it.

"You said your father was remarried. That must have been a rough time for you."

Amy found a shaky laugh. "It still is. I can't stand to go home, Adam. To see Kay in my mother's kitchen—using my mother's recipes because Dad likes them—I just hate it."

After he'd digested her words, Adam asked, "What's she like? Quite frankly, she seemed nice enough on the phone. Of course, appearances can be deceiving—"

"No," Amy stopped him, forcing herself to be honest. "She's just as nice as she can be. She's never done a single thing to make me feel the way I do. In fact, she's bent over backwards to make her peace with me. But I just can't let go with her—I can't let her in. I feel awful about it, but—I'm like a record stuck in a glitch."

Silently Adam reached over and took her hand. As always, his touch sent chills of apprehension and delight racing up and down her body. There was magic in his fingers, but healing warmth as well, and she wondered for the hundredth time in the last few hours which of the two he wanted most to give her. She hoped it was both.

"Are you tired of being unhappy, Amy? Are you ready to move on?"

There it was again—his "let me help you" voice. Amy was trying to figure out if Davis was too far from San Francisco to pull off a Saturday night date, and Adam was still trying to get her to tackle the piano in the chapel! Suddenly resentful, Amy removed her hand and stared at him. "I'm tired of you bringing this up every time we're alone together, Adam," she told him truthfully. "You've made it very clear you're more than willing to listen to my troubles. Sooner or later I'll probably end up babbling all over you. But right now, couldn't we just enjoy the sunshine and the chance to get to know each other?"

Adam pulled back and met her eyes. "You really believe in calling a spade a spade, don't you, Amy?"

"I respect you too much to play games, Adam," she told him, uncomfortable with the turn of events. "I know you're worried about me, but I also get the feeling that you have at least one other motive for wanting to get to know me better."

Amy never knew for sure where those ill-timed words came from. Maybe it was the clear mountain air, the need to escape all his searching questions about her flight from her family and the Lord. Maybe it was just the message in his eyes that his cautious words could not conceal; maybe it was a desire to replace his memory of Linda with a heart-picture that framed only Amy's face. But the fencing, the starting and stopping, the mixed messages, all seemed to come to a head in that awkward moment.

With an effort that Amy was sure cost him dearly, Adam pulled his eyes, then his hand, away from hers and rose to his feet. He gathered all the corn dog remnants and paper trash from the table and stuffed it in the nearest bin. Then, still without looking at her, he motioned toward the door.

"I'm eager to get to know all the counselors here this week, Amos," he declared, deliberately using her camp name. "If I have to come in to town again tomorrow, I think I'll bring Trevor Grant along. I'm having more than a little trouble figuring him out. Aren't you?"

Amy stood up and faced him squarely. She chose her words with care. "Yes, Adam. I'm having a lot of trouble figuring him out. Sometimes he acts like a man who really desires me as a woman, and sometimes he acts like he only wants me as a friend."

"Perhaps . . . ," Adam stared slowly, his eyes now boring into hers, " . . . he has a terribly good reason for his vacillation that he's not at liberty to explain."

89

"Surely he knows that I'd rather hear it straight, Adam, no matter how painful it might be."

"Painful for whom?" he countered, his tension rising. "What's a pinprick to you might be a sledge hammer to him, Amy." He did not try to smile. His blue eyes darkened with some kind of internal combat. "I'm sure I speak for Trevor when I say . . . let's just let it be."

In that instant, Amy was sure of only two things: neither one of them was speaking of Trevor Grant, and despite the strained command that Adam had just issued, he wasn't at all ready to just "let it be."

Neither was she.

CHAPTER 6

THERE WERE ONLY SEVEN AFTERNOON project groups, but nonetheless Amy was surprised at the turnout for her mini-choir in the bowl. Twenty-five eager young voices—including her little shadow, Julie Ann—were warming up under the intense afternoon sun, begging her to teach them every song she'd ever learned that was remotely suitable for Camp Colina! Cindy and Nathan, Joey's twin friends from home, arrived within minutes of each other, but Joey never showed up. Secretly, Amy was pleased. She had to assume that he was making new friends.

"Okay, guys, I'll teach you all I know," she promised the children when they were all assembled. "But just a few a day so we can really learn them. And I want you to give some thought to which song you like best because I think we ought to sing one on the last night's service, kind of like a choir. Would you like that?"

She was inundated with an enthusiastic chorus that was more than enough inspiration to give up an afternoon by the pool. Once she started to warm up, the songs filled her mind and her heart, and Amy hardly thought of anything else.

Tiffany, sullen and silent, perched on a log just far enough away to make clear her refusal to join the group . . . but entirely too close to convince Amy that she really wanted to stay away. After all, there were six other places she could have chosen to spend her afternoon—not counting the pool or some distant hiding place of her own devising. Tiffany had been the first person Amy had encountered when she'd returned from her trip with Adam, and underneath the sulky silence, Amy was certain she'd seen a glimmer of relief.

She could have used some relief herself. Her trip with Adam had been unsettling. He had remained warm and open on the way back, the same sterling Adam Reed that seemed to the foundation of his very character. There had been no further mention of "Trevor" or any reference to Amy's unresolved spiritual dilemma. Yet Amy was frankly puzzled by his words and inconsistent behavior. She knew she couldn't force him into any more personal revelations, but she also knew that there was no way in the world she could gather up her conflicting feelings for the man and stuff them into a duffle bag until the week was over.

Nonetheless they'd had a pleasant shopping expedition, and Amy had returned with everything she really wanted except for a swimming suit. Of course, she'd found a large, plain one in her goodwill bag the night before, but after an hour spent in Adam's cautious platonic company, she was yearning, womanlike, to have at least one piece of clothing in her wardrobe that might elicit the same thousand watt smile he'd given her the first time they met. Hiking boots and baggy borrowed blue jeans were definitely not the ticket to elegance!

By late afternoon Amy was hoarse but happy. The

92

kids had a lot of potential as a choral group—not to mention enthusiasm—and she was certain that with a few more days of practice she'd be ready to have them do the "anthem" for the closing night's service. It was as near as she'd ever come to admitting that she rather liked the memory of her own solo days. But she'd come back to the camp as a counselor, not an eager child, and it was her turn to lead the children, not be one.

It was outrageously hot by four o'clock, and Amy was enormously grateful for Adam's thoughtful decision, relayed through the camp right after lunch, that all staff meetings would be held in the pool as soon as the kids cleared out for dinner! Even a brief dip would be preferable to a whole afternoon of unrelieved heat.

Of course Amy had barely closed the pool gate behind her when Joey began to shriek her name.

"Hey, Amy, where you been all day? You wanna see me dive? Look at this!"

Amazed at his untiring energy, Amy grinned and applauded. "You're getting better every minute. I'm afraid to show you how I get into the pool."

"How?"

Smugly she marched down the steps. "Easy, huh?"

"Chicken!" He smacked the water in her direction, and she splashed him back. Several of his cabinmates joined in the fun, but Tiffany, lurking alone in the shallow end, made no attempt to join the merriment.

"Whoa! Enough for me!" Amy finally capitulated, crawling out for a breather on the steps near the quiet girl. "You're smart to hide over here, Tiff."

"I'm not hiding," Tiffany retorted. "I just don't like the boys to splash me."

Amy smiled. It was *almost* a conversation. "I'm not sure I do either, Tiffany, but sometimes I just play along because it makes them happy. At least it's hot enough that I don't mind getting my hair wet. It's hard to believe how cold it can get up here at night when it's like this all afternoon!"

"It would be colder if you didn't have a sleeping bag," Tiffany commented, not looking at Amy. "You're lucky somebody brought you one."

It could almost have been an expression of concern. Tiffany, of all the girls, had been in a position to notice that when Amy had first arrived she'd had no gear at all.

"You're absolutely right. Adam made sure I had everything I needed."

"You mean 'Summit,'" Tiffany corrected her. "You can't call the grownups by their own names up here."

Amy nodded, but refused to rephrase her statement. Ever since Adam had told her the roots of his nickname, she'd decided that she'd call him Adam and nothing else.

When Tiffany called a halt to the conversation by trotting off to sunbathe, Amy went back in the water and tried to do laps—a virtual impossibility with the moving obstacle course represented by the children. She ended up using her few precious minutes in the pool with Joey, who had arbitrarily decided that today, of all days, he would learn to float. He chattered incessantly, reciting every moment of his day as though they'd been apart for weeks instead of hours. Amy discovered that the advent of Grand Slam's afternoon baseball group had been what kept him from clinging to her during music time. She decided it had been a wise move on Adam's part not to put Joey in her Bible class.

"I take it you're glad you came," she declared, tongue in cheek, while she braced his back near the surface of the water. "Who are your special buddies?"

He wriggled all over. "They're all my special buddies! We do everything together!"

"And . . . the Giraffe? Is he fun to be with?" Quite frankly, Amy still had her doubts about the man.

94

Joey shrugged. "He's all right. He doesn't laugh as much as Dad does."

Amy had to smile at the unfair comparison. Nobody laughed as much as Bill Shelby did! He had a round, hairless face that grew red when he was excited; before her mother died he had regularly laughed until he'd hugged his stomach and gasped for breath. Surely Joey had seen this side of her father by now, but Amy had to admit that she hadn't seen him too relaxed since he'd married Kay.

"Joey," she asked thoughtfully, "Does it seem to you that Dad . . . laughs more or less when I'm around?"

Joey pondered that for a minute. "He laughs when he plays with me. And sometimes when Mama teases him. When you're there everybody just talks like grownups. How come?"

Amy didn't really want to answer that. She had to wonder, though, how much strain she put on the family when she was feeling morose. She couldn't remember having a very good time at home since her father's remarriage, but then again she'd done precious little to contribute to a convivial atmosphere during her rare and unenthusiastic visits. She surprised herself by asking, "Does your mother ever get silly like Daddy does?"

Joey cackled and thwacked the water. "She's worse than he is! When the two of them go crazy I'm the one who has to act like a grownup!"

Of course. How could my father have married a woman without a sense of humor? A week ago she would have said, how could he have married anyone at all? But suddenly that idea seemed a bit ridiculous. *How much you've influenced me already, Adam.*

By now she knew that she wanted to be changed. She wanted the healing that Adam had to offer—and she wanted Adam. But she wasn't at all certain just what it was he wanted from her. One minute he acted like a Father Confessor, and the next he gave every indication of a man who wanted to lose himself in Amy's thick black hair. She'd already gone out on a limb and hinted that she might be interested in getting to know him a great deal better, and she wasn't about to stick her foot in her mouth again until Adam made his next move. And, despite his indecipherable references to secrecy and "sledge hammer pain," the woman in Amy was absolutely sure that sooner or later, he *would* make the next move.

Of course, she knew it would be smarter to do as he asked and forget the whole thing. But as she caught sight of his well-tanned body approaching the pool in modest blue trunks with a red and white towel draped around his shoulders, she realized—with sudden, piercing clarity—that it was already far too late for such wisdom.

He was not alone. Trevor Grant strolled along beside him, engaged in urgent conversation. Adam's eyes never left the other man's face until he finished speaking and both of them plunged into the deep end of the pool.

Amy only saw one of them hit the water. It wasn't as though only one of them reappeared and soared off the diving board; it was just that the sandy-haired, long lean body arrested her senses so fully as it knifed the water that she never really noticed what happened after that. Suddenly her borrowed suit seemed shabby and too large and too small all at the same time . . . and certainly out of date as well, although she couldn't seem to remember what style of swimming suit was in fashion at the moment. Her eyes massaged his muscled chest for several moments before he turned, suddenly, and met her searching gaze.

A sharp little gasp, somewhere between delight and pain, unbottled itself from her throat as Adam stared at her. Her small floating brother seemed like a useless subterfuge; she wanted to hide herself in the water. She ached to escape, to break this unscheduled gaze of mutual longing. *Let me go, Adam,* her eyes begged him. *Don't embarrass me in front of everyone.*

But he would not—could not?—look away. An ache . . . a shudder . . . seemed to pass through him. Amy felt the same painful, joyful shiver in her own heart. Then someone—Trevor?—dived into the pool, kicking three feet of water into Adam's face. In slow motion he seemed to feel the splash, acknowledge the presence of others, and release his eyes from her gaze.

"That's it!" the young lifeguard called. "Kids out! Hustle it up! Time to get ready for dinner. Cook said to remind you that it's Raccoon Cabin's turn to set up the tables. Let's go!"

For several minutes the jumble of tiny bodies ruptured the water and the air waves and none of the adults tried to speak.

"Could everybody just sort of gather together down here in the shallow end?" Adam asked as the chaos faded, moving away from Amy with sure, steady strokes. She watched him for a second, still a bit dazed, before she pulled herself up on the side of the pool and crossed her legs, squaw-style, in readiness for her first camp staff meeting.

"So—how did it go today?" Adam asked when they were all assembled. "Anybody lost, confused, or ready to throw in the towel?"

He did not look at Trevor, Amy noticed, but he did swivel his head just once to glance in her direction. She said nothing.

The counselor who'd read her testimony that morning was the first to comment. "I don't think we should have started off with the prodigal son. I would rather have seen an adult as the errant soul instead of a child."

Adam nodded, honoring her feeling. "One of the counselors tried to expand the story and consider it from the point of view of a child forgiving a grownup. You might want to present it that way tomorrow."

"With role playing," another man added.

"What a wonderful idea!" Amy burst out, not even knowing where her thoughts were leading her. "We could assign a group to act out each parable we study this week and present them to the whole group on Friday night."

"That's twenty groups, Amy," Trevor said.

She met his eyes for the first time that evening—wondering whose side he was on—while Adam mused, "Good point, Trev. But Amy has a good idea. Maybe we could do just one parable a night at the bowl—the one we studied that day. A group or leader could volunteer, or I could just wing it with whatever children liked the idea."

"I think we need a small group to start," Amy insisted. "This is a junior camp, after all. Most of this is new to them."

Unfortunately her eyes fell on Trevor on the last line. Defensively he countered, "It's new to me too but that doesn't mean I'm not willing to give it a shot."

"Super!" Grand Slam shouted, clapping his hands. "Let's let the counselors act out the prodigal. By tomorrow the kids will be begging to do it."

"Good idea, Grand Slam," Adam concurred. "Everybody who wants to be part of that just come to the bowl fifteen minutes early tonight, okay? We'll rough it out from there."

Several heads nodded in agreement before Adam changed the subject. "Any other problems? Food, cabins, other assignments? Any kids with special needs I may have missed?" Carefully he glanced at each face, acknowledged the caution in Amy's with the barest hint of a nod, then moved on again. "I'd like to ask your opinion about Holy Communion. Some camps have it every night and some only once

. . . like the last night. I think it's vital for the kids to have this experience here and frankly, I'm tempted to start this evening.''

"No."

Everybody looked around to see who had uttered that single word, and to Amy's surprise their faces were all focused on her. Had she really spoken out loud? Desperately she tried to shield the chaos Adam's sincerity caused within her. "I just . . . just think they're too young for Communion. They're just starting to learn about camp life, let alone Jesus. It would just be a game to them. Some of them aren't even baptized yet. I just—" She cut off when she met Adam's eyes. He wasn't going to oppose her, but she knew that for every excuse she had voiced out loud, he realized that she had another two or three buried deep in her heart. *She* wasn't ready to take Communion, not by a long shot. She could hardly explain her reticence to two hundred eager young campers.

Much to her relief, support for her point of view arrived unexpectedly from Pinky Ferris. "Amy's got a point," the cheerful blond backed her up. "I think we need to build up to something like that . . . prepare them little by little so the Sacrament has some kind of meaning.''

"They'll be taking their cues from us," Adam said simply. "Communion has great meaning for me."

After that nobody commented for a while. Trevor licked his lips and stared at Adam, his face a cry for help. Amy couldn't help but echo his feeling in her heart. Again she wondered how much of the man lay below the surface. Was it possible she had misjudged him?

When it became obvious that no one else had anything to say, Adam rose with a handful of quiet words. "Could we all join hands and have a moment's prayer?''

Instantly they came around him, some in the pool

and some beside it, holding hands in two semi-circles with Adam more or less attached to both.

"Heavenly Father, give us your blessing as we lead these young people. Thank you for this first successful day in Your service. Continue to lead us as You see fit. Help us to grow in wisdom and patience, understanding and acceptance. Guide us in Jesus' path." He paused for a long moment while the woman on Amy's right squeezed her hand. "Amen."

They bounced apart, noting the time, scurrying toward their cabins before the dinner bell sounded. Amy was quick to grab her towel and disappear with the others, but a single word stopped her.

"Amy."

She didn't want to look at him. She didn't want to be alone with him right then, trying to hide from all the feelings he aroused within her. But she couldn't ignore the simple plea in his voice. Maybe he was ready to talk. Ready to give her some hope . . . or at least tell her the truth. She stood very still as he called over the hubbub, "Do you have a moment to go over the music for this evening?"

"Of course," she tossed back, quickly planning the service so there would be no need for discussion if music was the only thing on his mind. "I've got some ideas that I hope will meet with your approval."

He slung a towel over his shoulder and approached her slowly. By the time he reached her side they were alone beside the pool. "I have the utmost of faith in you," he declared. "The music is entirely in your hands."

"Thank you," she whispered, wondering what he had in mind. Despite those few moments of visual fireworks in the pool, he seemed deadly serious now. More than likely he was worried about her reluctance to take Communion and was planning to use it as a lever to get her to confess her adolescent folly. Uncertainly she asked, "What did you really want to talk to me about?"

100

He ran a nervous hand through his hair. It was a gesture she'd only seen him use when they were alone. In public he always looked unflappably calm.

"Two things, really. The first is something I presume you don't want to talk about in front of Trevor. Tiffany."

Amy was surprised. She didn't think he'd had any contact with the girl. "She's a real tough case, Adam. I've tried being tender; I've tried playing hardball; I've tried treating her as a peer. She's still at camp, but only on the surface."

"On the surface?"

"I've gotten her to go wherever she's supposed to go, but she'd determined to sit on the sidelines. She won't smile, won't talk—well, maybe just a sentence or two—and probably isn't listening, either. Half the time I have to act like a prison warden and the other half I just want to hold her in my arms. Underneath all those thorns there's a little girl in there just crying out for love, and I can't seem to find a way to give her any."

"She came to your music group today and that's strictly voluntary," Adam offered with predictable optimism. "That's got to be a good omen."

Amy was surprised that he knew that tidbit of information. She hadn't seen him all afternoon! But she answered simply, "She still had to sit off by herself. She's a hard worker, though. She almost seemed to enjoy the trail detail this morning."

Adam nodded. "I'm praying for her, Amy. I think she'll bloom. And I trust your instincts completely. Frankly, I'm a little more concerned about Trevor."

"Trevor?"

"He's in way over his head. He needs this camp but he's in no condition to be a counselor. I'm co-leading his Bible group, but I can't take over his cabin duties." He paused and looked at her directly. "You're his family group partner, Amy. I'm counting on you to keep him out of trouble."

"What makes you think I'm in any better shape than he is? I'm a spiritual basket case!"

He shook his head in quick denial. "You're a strong, loving, searching woman. You're going to be okay. You know what you want and sooner or later you'll find a way to get it. I'm concerned for you," he reached out to stroke her still damp cheek, "but I'm not worried."

She looked away, trembling in the face of his praise. *You're doing it to me again*, she wanted to whisper. *Your words belong to the camp director, but those hands that keep finding their way back to my face belong to a man who wants me.*

As if he could read her mind, Adam suddenly dropped his hand and tugged his towel against the back of his neck. "I think you can help Trevor," he forced out, surprising her with his insistent return to the topic. "Just listen to him. Help him understand that he's not alone. It's okay to be . . . searching."

"I'm not sure I'm the best person to give that assignment to," Amy reiterated a little more gently.

"Why is that?"

"In the first place, despite your confidence in me, I can hardly find my own trail here at the moment, let alone somebody else's. In the second place, it'll be hard for me to convince Tiffany I'm on her side if she knows I'm her father's confidante." She breathed deeply. "In the third place, Trevor's behavior with me, as I told you at lunch, is unpredictable at best, beastly at worst. He's not going to respond to any suggestions I make that sound like I'm backing you up."

He looked surprised. "Why is that?"

Amy wasn't prepared for the question; she certainly wasn't prepared to give the answer. But she swallowed hard and told him the truth. "He keeps insinuating that you and I are . . . romantically involved."

102

This time there was no disguising the lash of pain that whipped across Adam's face. He tore his eyes away from hers and straightened as the first evening breeze stole across the pool. Tension plundered the space between them as the dinner gong clanged at the top of the rise.

"Better nip that rumor in the bud, Amos," he declared with forced levity, careful to keep his eyes trained on Persistence Peak. "You wouldn't want the whole camp to know I have a weakness for long, black hair."

For hours those words echoed in Amy's heart. Half of her was certain that Adam had actually been flirting with her; the other half was sure his flip answer concealed a very definite "No" to Trevor's implications. She couldn't think of any safe way to ferret out the truth.

"Are you . . . heading on over to the bowl?" Trevor asked her after supper. He'd eaten with Adam, just close enough for Amy to watch the two of them but too far away to eavesdrop. She was dying to know what words had been exchanged.

"Yes. I'm not sure what's going to happen with this . . . role playing, but I thought I'd be on hand just in case Adam's short on volunteers."

Trevor fell into step beside her, his stride awkward on the dusty trail. "I . . . really like the way you sing, Amy. The kids are so excited."

She tried to smile—he was trying to be civil, after all, and Adam had asked her to be nice to him— before she announced, "Tiffany came to my afternoon group today, Trevor."

A heavy shadow framed his face as he looked away. "She hasn't . . . she hasn't said more than two words to me since we got here."

Amy laid a hand on his arm. "She hasn't said much more than that to me either, but I've kept talking to her just the same. If you let her slip away she'll just keep reiterating that you don't care about her. You've got to find a way to change her mind."

Trevor shook his head and stuck both hands in the stiff pockets of his new designer jeans. "I'm swimming upstream, Amy. I ran away when I should have stayed, and now I've got to earn the right to come back."

Amy wanted to ask him just what he meant, but she knew that he, like Tiffany, would tell her when the time was right.

He grimaced at his own predicament. "I couldn't believe how hard that prodigal story hit me this morning. Unfortunately real life doesn't have too much to do with parables, does it?"

"Oh, Trevor, you're wrong!" Amy heard herself saying. "Real life is nothing *but* parables! Do you think Jesus made them up just to entertain people?"

He tried to laugh. "No, I think he made them up to bewilder new camp counselors on their first day of Bible class."

Amy shared the joke, then asked directly, "Was Adam much help?"

He rolled his eyes. "He *taught* the class. I just watched. I don't have any idea what I would have done if he hadn't taken over."

"I'm sure you would have done just fine. Did he help you prepare for tomorrow?"

"Yes, but he's still going to be there if I get in a jam. I . . . I think the kids would be better off if I just kept my mouth shut."

"I doubt it," Amy refuted. "Besides, knowing Adam, he won't let you hide in your corner for long. In a day or two he won't come to your class at all, Trevor. Once he thinks you're ready, you'll be on your own." Too late she realized she had just added fuel to Trevor's fire, revealing how well she understood their leader.

But to her surprise Trevor nodded amiably, then said in an undertone, "Adam . . . set me straight about . . . some things, Amy. I guess he just . . . needed to spend some . . . extra time with you at first since you took over your step-mother's place at the last minute and I . . . took it all wrong." He met her eyes apologetically. "I'm trying to take my size twelves out of my mouth again, Amy. I'm sorry."

Amy was sorry too. Not just because Trevor had accused her of having a romantic relationship with Adam—but because apparently Trevor was wrong. She wanted to ask if Adam had clarified this point before or after their little chat by the pool, but she couldn't think of a good way to ask. "Let's just forget it, Trevor. But just for the record . . . even if I were interested in Adam, or anybody else up here . . . it's really no reason for you to treat me like a pariah, you know."

He looked at her soberly. "You're trying to tell me that I'm barking up the wrong tree."

"I'm trying to tell you I'd like to be your friend. But I've got enough problems to work out at this camp without adding . . . confusing relationships to the picture."

He didn't really look convinced, but at least he was willing to go along with her request. "Okay. I could really do with a genuine friend up here." When he tossed an arm around her shoulder for a quick platonic hug, Amy managed to return the embrace. It seemed like the perfect way to finish the discussion . . . until she realized that they'd just reached the top of the bowl and Adam, at the bottom, was quietly watching them.

He eyes were dark, assessing, but he turned away too quickly for Amy to tell if he were applauding or condemning her action. It was hardly a time for personal worries or challenges; the bowl was already full of counselors and a number of stray children from different cabins.

"Okay, folks," Adam called out to no one in particular. "There are enough of us here to start. I thought we'd pick a father, two sons, some herdsmen—"

"A fatted calf," Grand Slam added.

"And I think the son should be a daughter," his wife chimed in. "Just to make it all more ... universal."

"In that case I'll be the mother," Amy declared, suddenly afraid that Adam would try to make her the prodigal.

It was Trevor, in the end, who volunteered for that unlucky position. Adam looked so pleased that she suspected that the two of them had arranged a plan of some kind over dinner. She was not surprised when he suggested, "What if we ... did it once the regular way, just the way Jesus told it ... to set the stage. Then we could ... try these other *avant garde* demonstrations later and hope the kids would get the point."

He turned to Amy and murmured *sotto voce*, "I'd like to be the father this time around, if you don't mind. I think it would be easier for Trevor this way." His eyes asked for her understanding. *I'm not pushing you out of the way, Amy. I'm trying to heal this broken man.*

"No problem," she readily agreed. "I'll play any part you want except the prodigal. I won't get any healing done with an audience, Adam."

He looked surprised. "I would never do that to you, Amy. I know you think I've pressed you too hard, but only when we've been alone. In public I always uphold you as a leader. Most of these people already consider you my assistant."

I don't want to be your assistant, her eyes flashed. *I want to be your woman.* For an instant she was absolutely certain that he could read her mind. His face was torn with frustration, determination, and tightly leashed desire; his eyes drilled hers with such intensity that she was certain he would speak, ending her confusion once and for all.

Instead he turned away and started giving orders to his "players." There was an edge to his voice she'd never heard before. In another man, she would have called it anger.

"Okay, kids," he announced a few minutes later. "I'd like you to watch how this is done, and when the next group comes up a child can play a grownup role or vice versa. How does that sound?"

She knew he had visions of Tiffany volunteering, but Amy knew better than to hope. The girl sat stiffly beside her during the first episode, commenting only once when her father, the prodigal, begged Adam for forgiveness.

"I don't know what he thinks he's doing," she growled under breath. "He's not a kid and none of us lives in the Bible."

"And none of us can live without forgiveness, Tiffany. We've all made mistakes we wish we could do over."

"Even you?" The girl's tone was disbelieving.

"Even me." Amy met Tiffany's eyes squarely. "Especially me. There's one night of my life I'd give anything at all to do over again."

"One night?" Tiffany whispered, her eyes dark and sad. "How can you . . . how can you change something like that?"

Amy shook her head. "I can't, Tiffany. I can only ask God to forgive me. But if . . . if the person I hurt were still alive, I'd go to her and beg for *her* forgiveness. I'd do everything in my power to take away the wounds I gave her."

She was guessing, of course, knowing as little as she did about the Grant's family life. But Tiffany was watching her so intently that Amy was sure she'd struck a nerve.

107

"Do you . . . do you think she'd forgive you if you really did such a terrible thing?" The frowning child asked. "What did you do, Amos?"

Amy closed her eyes, oblivious to the ongoing mini-drama at the front of the bowl. She couldn't answer the last question, but maybe if she answered the first well enough, Tiffany would let her get away with it. "Yes, I think she'd forgive me, Tiffy, because she was my mother. And mothers and fathers and children always find a way to forgive each other. That's what being a family is all about."

Tiffany held her gaze for several moments before she turned her eyes back to the clearing where little red-headed Cindy was playing the role of the "mother" in a modified version of the parable. Trevor edged back up to Amy's side and whispered tersely, "Whose side are you on? Why did you make Tiffany talk to you the whole time I was up there? I wanted her to get the point! Adam said it was really important that I stick my neck out."

Despite the anger in his voice, he looked so harried that Amy told him, "I think she got the point. Maybe not quite the way you and Adam had in mind, but . . . trust me, Trevor, your performance was not in vain."

"You're sure?"

She smiled. "As sure as one can ever be with Tiffany."

All their visions for role-playing the parables came true that night. The acting and the prayer and discussion that followed turned out to be the entire service, without any of Amy's scheduled music at all! Before they were done almost every child and counselor had taken some role—even if it was just a guest at the celebration—and the sense of camp kinship had multiplied tenfold. Tiffany, of course, hadn't budged an inch, and Julie Ann had opted to keep the log warm beside her.

When they gathered around for Adam's closing

108

prayer, he was too far away from Amy to see her face, or give her any directions. Yet she knew precisely when and what he wanted her to sing as they strolled back to the meadow. This time it was "Kum Ba Yah," an old African spiritual that would keep them humming all the way to bed.

Adam hugged a dozen people good night—kids and counselors—but Amy was not one of them. The campers separated happily, peacefully, with the Timber Wolf girls and Grizzly boys flanking Amy and Trevor all the way back to their cabins. They moved in a little closer when the coyotes began to howl, but they all felt too good to be afraid.

When they reached Grizzly Cabin, Joey gave Amy an enormous hug and slobbery kiss. Moved by the familial tenderness, Trevor spoke softly to his daughter.

"Goodnight, sweetheart. See you in the morning."

When the stiff-lipped girl said nothing, Amy whispered, "Your daddy said goodnight, Tiff. I guess you didn't hear him."

Cautiously Tiffany looked at Amy, then at Trevor. A strange palette of emotions washed over her face. For an instant Amy thought she might duplicate Joey's enthusiastic hug, but that hope died as she deliberately moved out of her father's reach.

But before she'd gone more that a step or two, the little girl tossed a scrawny handful of words in his direction.

"Goodnight, Daddy."

Her voice was too soft to be heard by any but the most determined of loving parents, so Amy wasn't even sure that Trevor heard his daughter's ever so tentative offering of peace.

Still, it was a beginning.

CHAPTER 7

AMY WOKE UP THE NEXT MORNING feeling light-hearted and full of Grace. Morning was always her best time, but she was certain that today was going to be special. Her breakthroughs the day before had all been tiny— with Tiffany, with Trevor, with her acceptance of her new family—but now that these doors were open, she was confident that more progress would be appreciable day by day.

Once again she'd gone to sleep with Adam's Bible in her hand, almost feeling his presence because she knew he'd loaned her the single thing he valued most. She still couldn't open it, but she mentally recalled snatches of all her favorite verses as she lay in her bunk, especially the parables she knew they'd study later in the week. Every work of Scripture that Adam had mentioned was still etched in her mind, and she knew that when she finally did open the Bible, these would be the passages she'd seek out first. She was certain that Adam knew it, too.

On this glistening, dew-drop morning, even his hesitation about the true nature of their relationship had become clearer to Amy. There was just no way on earth that she'd imagined all of those tender, searing moments; he had to be feeling some of her hunger. Their communication was too perfect—even when it was wordless—to hinge on banal attributes of leadership and song. They were like joggers who were still evenly paced on the last mile or a marathon; members of a jazz band who'd jammed together for years. It couldn't have happened by accident.

She had two theories for Adam's hesitation. It was entirely possible that he was shy. On the surface he was as outgoing and open as a man could be, but in the secret reaches of his heart, he might well be a cautious suitor—an all or nothing kind of man. His very sensitivity might be the result of some long ago pain, and the major heartbreak right there.

His role at Camp Colina would also restrict him; he wasn't the sort of man who would take advantage of his position. Several of Adam's private comments could be taken to mean that he didn't consider it proper for the camp director to be dating one of his counselors.

This was a point of view Amy could appreciate, but she refused to let their respective positions preclude a romance that could very well be the most important one in her life. If he wanted to wait until the week was over to redefine their relationship, she could handle that. She could wait. She loved his discretion, his compassion, his integrity. She didn't want to make him uncomfortable, nor did she want to complicate his life in this new and challenging job. But she didn't want to give him up, either, and one way or another, she'd have to make that clear to him.

He was waiting for her by the trail at daybreak. It was possible, of course, that Adam would have gone hiking this morning anyway and just happened to see her cross the meadow, but Amy thrust the thought from her mind. There were plenty of trails that led away from the lodge; he wouldn't have had trouble finding solitude at dawn if that's what he'd been seeking.

"Top o' the morning, m'lady," he greeted her, tipping his nonexistent derby as she approached him. "Lovely day, Miss Shelby. Don't you agree?"

Thrilled to find him in the same buoyant mood that she herself was in, Amy tossed him a grin that concealed not one iota of her feelings. "An exquisite day, Mr. Reed. No doubt about it."

"*Doctor* Reed, if you please," he corrected her, still grinning. "If we're going to be formal let's at least be accurate."

Amy laughed. "I thought the only doctors in Davis were veterinarians."

"Not a chance. Although I must admit it's a great place to be sick as a dog."

They groaned together at the lame joke, which took hilarious proportions in their mutually playful mood.

"Boy, I'm hungry!" Adam told her. "I'm not used to eating on a schedule. The food here in great but I'm tempted to get a hot plate and cooler for my periodic junk food binges." He gave her a sideways glance. "Can you cook corn dogs?"

The question stirred sudden domestic urges within her, and Amy longed to display her culinary talents with stuffed zucchini and homemade wheat berry bread. "I've never tried," she answered lightly. ". . . but my popcorn and chocolate chip cookies are sensational."

"Ah, a woman after my own heart. Irene made me some cookies right after I got here, but the new cook doesn't indulge me very much."

"How is Irene?" Amy asked. "I wish I could see her."

Adam gestured toward Persistence Peak. "Be my guest. They've been alone up there long enough that I don't imagine they'd be averse to a little company."

Amy shook her head. "I'd feel like I was intruding. Besides, I doubt if they'd even remember me. I was just one of hundreds of kids that poured through here—"

"And they loved every one of you. I've heard more old stories about this kid and that since I've been here than you could believe. I could write a book called *How They Spent Their Summer Vacation*."

"Sounds great, Adam, but nobody who'd ever taken an English composition class would want to read it. What scintillating topic did you pick for your dissertation?"

He chuckled, then tickled her side. "You'll pay for that, lady."

Amy squealed just once, as he wanted her to, then settled down to pace her steps to his long-legged stride. She was all but bouncing off the trail. Yesterday at lunch had been nice, but so serious compared to this joyous morning! Her confidence was bouncing off the walls of all conscious reason.

And then, out of nowhere, she heard Adam's Father Confessor voice.

"Amy—"

"Don't you dare!" She turned on him with mock fury. "We're having a positively marvelous time this morning and I will *not* have you spoil it with your maudlin psychological ploys to get me to—"

"Maudlin psychological ploys?" He barely got the words out before he burst out laughing. Even his dimples seemed to be laughing at her! "What kind of a description is—"

"Oh, come on, Adam!" she chastised him, returned his earlier tickle with a jab in the ribs. "You know I'll tell you when I'm ready. Can't you wait till some dark night when I'm good and depressed?"

He stopped in the middle of the trail and turned to face her. His eyes grew sober; his hands found their way to her hair. "Amy, honey," he said gently, using

113

the endearment for the first time, "I'm trying to spare you any more dark nights. I'm trying to free you from any more bouts of this soul-crippling depression. Please help me a little bit."

His concern ate away at her sense of humor, and she studied the ground, fighting the urge to pull away. Over and over again he'd done this to her. It was almost as thought her salvation was more important to Adam than it was to Amy herself! Secretly she knew she had to get her confession out of the way. It was bad enough that her anguish had kept her from God, kept her from Kay, kept her from her father and her own peace of mind. She was not about to let it keep her from Adam.

"I think it was rotten of you to do this now when we were both in such a good mood," she declared, tossing out her last shield of resistance.

His fingertips tugged her hair back from her face and nested in the small hollow at the base of her neck. "I didn't think it would hurt so much right now." He began to knead the sensitive skin beneath his hands. His breathing grew uneven. "It's like going to the dentist, honey. It's awfully scary, but you can't start getting better until he pulls out that bad tooth."

Ever so slowly he put his arms around her in the most platonic of caring gestures. Amy leaned against him, fighting a sudden urge to weep. It was crazy. She'd known this man less than two whole days, yet he had maneuvered a trail past all of her defenses, offering her reunion with the Lord and a clean heart with the gentlest of persuasion. It was uncanny how close she felt to him; how special their understanding, right from the start. Suddenly she knew. She could tell him. After all these years, somehow he would make it all right.

She lifted her glistening eyes to face him and gushed out her story in quick, broken phrases. He held her close and never said a word.

"When I first went to college, I just . . . sort of went crazy, I guess. I was so rebellious, so angry . . . I know lots of kids are like that, but . . . when I met Kirk it seemed so important to assert myself. There were so many things he wanted me to do that I knew my parents thought were wrong. And I didn't . . . I never did very many of them, but I wanted to. Just to prove it was Amy thinking, Amy growing up."

She stopped for a moment. Mutely Adam waited, the circle of his arms ever so gently offering comfort. "Then I . . . joined a sorority. And they sent . . . they sent invitations to all the parents for some celebration . . . and mother came. I didn't want her to. I didn't ask her to. I wanted to go to San Francisco with Kirk to see a rock concert. He already had the tickets! And he was so angry when I tried to cancel . . . said it was such a big deal and I was such a baby to care what my parents thought. So, I," she gulped, losing control of her voice, "I went! I made it crystal clear that I didn't want her there! I just said hello and goodbye and left her there in my room, all alone! I felt awful, but I did it, Adam!" She broke down again, and Adam, not knowing the end of the tale but not needing to, held her closer yet. She cried for a few more minutes, then slowly calmed. She stood back to face him while she finished.

"I never saw her again. She was too hurt and ashamed to stay there. It was already late and it was a long drive home but she left as soon as she could pack." Amy didn't need to finish the story; the ending was engraved in her eyes. "Don't tell me anybody could have had an accident, because not anybody did. My mother did . . . because she was tired and upset and ashamed of her only daughter. She had a right to be ashamed! And I'm still ashamed."

Her voice faded away. Vaguely she felt Adam's hands rubbing her shoulders. The motion seemed to caress her heart. But after a moment she turned and started up the trail, unable to face him just then. He didn't try to make her talk, but he reached out for her hand and kneaded it with warm and quiet fingers as they walked.

Together they padded the dusty path in pristine silence for at least a mile before he questioned, "Better?"

Amy nodded and slowly met his eyes. "I've never been able to tell anyone before." She managed to smile at him, unable to mask the relief that his silent caring had brought her. She wanted to tell him how special she thought he was . . . how special their silent communion was. It was as though they were destined for this moment. For more than this moment. For a future so perfect that words would be redundant. . . .

She knew now that before the week was out, Adam would heal all her wounds; she only hoped she could do the same for him. But it seemed a bit gushy to say all this, so instead she tried to tease him. "You know, you're . . . very good at this sort of thing, Adam."

He smiled as he tossed an arm around her, equally eager to keep the tone light now that the worst was over. "First in my class in Empathy One-A at the seminary. They always said I'd go far."

It took Amy a moment to follow his words. "Seminary?" she forced out, shock all but paralyzing her sense of speech. "You went to . . . seminary?"

He grinned. "I tried to avoid it, I'll admit, but they weren't about to give me a doctorate in pastoral counseling unless I showed up for class."

Amy swallowed, stepping back so quickly that his hand fell off her shoulder. She could feel the red invade her face as the pathetic truth of the situation hit her. Empathy! Silent communion! A happily ever after! How could she have been so stupid? He was a pastor . . . a man trained to listen, trained to care . . . about anyone! She'd never known a man better suited to the ministry, nor more graced with integrity and

116

compassion. His concern for a stranger should have been to his credit, but to Amy's mind his profession was a betrayal of everything she thought had passed between them. He didn't care about her, Amy Shelby, person, friend . . . *woman*. She was a member of the flock . . . no more, no less. And suddenly, that was an untenable place to be.

"I've left the girls alone long enough, Adam," she blurted out with no pretense of grace. "I'd better hurry back to the cabin."

Before her eyes his face changed. His lighthearted tenderness turned gray and ashen. He looked at her like he'd never see her again . . . as though he, not Amy, had just confessed an unforgivable sin. She knew he didn't understand. Maybe someday she could explain it to him, but not right now. She didn't want to hurt him—she just couldn't bear the humiliation of his neutral compassion. She was drenched with the sudden, piercing knowledge that she wanted far, far more from Adam Reed than he had ever intended to give her. More than she had ever wanted from any man. Much more than she deserved.

She had to escape. She couldn't let him see the hole he'd ripped in her heart while he'd been trying so very hard to heal her. *I'm running away again,* some part of her protested, closing her eyes to the anguished look on his face. But the panic seized her, and she fled.

She hadn't gone three steps before Adam's voice, sharper than she'd ever heard it, commanded her to stop. "Not this time, Amy! For seven years you've been running away from God, running away from your father, running away from yourself! I won't be added to that cowardly list of excuses. No matter what you're feeling right now—no matter how angry or hurt or embarrassed you are—come back here and tell me! We've shared too much to pretend it never happened!" She turned back to face him, shame for

117

her cowardice now added to her list of gaping wounds. And then, incredibly, before she could speak, Adam whispered, "You can't possibly feel any worse than I do."

She studied his face in the silence of the tiny glen. He looked exactly the way she felt—confused, battered, torn wide open for anyone to see. *He* was hurting, too. It didn't make any sense.

"Amy, I've been a minister for six years. I don't know why you thought I wasn't, but I can guess why you're so upset that I am."

She wasn't at all sure she could tell him; but he didn't give her a chance.

"I'm used to people sugarcoating their words around me, wrapping my 'flawless morality' in robes of snow-white cotton. And I've seen that look on your face more than once when some poor fool made the mistake of treating me like a normal man before he 'discovered' that I wasn't." He glared at her. She had never seen him so angry. "Did you know that ministers don't make mistakes? They never get mad. They never feel hurt. They never have a single need the Lord can't fill on demand!" His fury was awesome. "I expected more from you, Amy! I thought you were a cut above the rest!"

She shook her head. He'd gotten it all wrong, every bit of her inane reaction. And there was only one way to make him feel any better, even though it would cost her dearly. She'd have to tell him the whole truth.

"Adam—"

"But you should have known I was a pastor right from the start! So was that truth just too awful to bear? Did it make you feel better to think of me as—"

"I didn't know!" she blurted out, saying anything to get him to stop. "I thought you were a teacher just like me. I thought you taught history at UC Davis!"

It did stop him. For several minutes he was speechless, rolling all their conversations over in his mind. At last he settled down on a boulder near her side and muttered, "Assuming that's true—illogical, but true—it doesn't account for the way you acted when you found out about my profession. If you had any faith in me at all, you would realize that I'd judge you no differently because I've been called to serve the Lord. A Christian is a Christian no matter what he does for a living. If I was a special friend as a history teacher, I ought to be a special friend as a pastor. But suddenly there's a dozen rows of pews between us, and I'm looking down at you from the top of my pulpit with a Bible in each hand." He glared at her. "And *you* put me up there, lady. I spend enough time in the heights with my parishoners—I don't need to be sanctified by my friends."

Feeling somehow broken inside, Amy moved toward him, settling down wordlessly at his side. Deliberately she put her arm around his shoulder in a platonic hug. She forced her need for him from her mind.

"Adam, I'm going to tell you the truth. It's going to hurt me, and you've got to promise not to laugh . . . but I'm going to tell you what really happened here. You've got the whole thing backwards."

His eyes met hers with tired sadness, then he stole her next words. "I'm sorry I yelled at you, Amy. It's not your fault I wanted you to be something you aren't."

Very carefully she asked, "What did you want me to be?"

For a long time his eyes swept her face and her exquisite black hair before he turned away and sighed in defeat. "It doesn't matter. Let's just bury the hatchet and get back to the meadow, okay? It's almost time for morning watch." Gracefully he escaped from her platonic embrace and stood up, then offered her a hand. Amy let him pull her to her feet, but she didn't release his fingers until he looked at her.

"You wanted me to share my grief with you because you're a compassionate man and I'm your friend and because . . . it's your job." She swallowed hard and pushed out the words. "But I told you because . . . I was . . . falling in love with you, Adam, and I—" she faltered, "I thought you felt the same way about me. When I found out that you were a minister, I realized that I'd misinterpreted almost everything that had happened between us. You gave me enough clues—I just ignored them. I wanted to believe that you wanted me. It never occurred to me that you would have listened to anybody just the way you listened to me. Quoted the same Scriptures, held the same hand, prayed for the same hurting soul. It's to your credit that you would have given me just as much attention if I'd been a pimply teenage boy or somebody's octogenarian grandma. You're wonderful at what you do, Adam, and if I were looking for a minister, you'd be at the very top of my list."

She looked away and tucked her hair behind her ears in a frightened, defensive gesture. "But that wasn't the role I had in mind for you, Adam," she breathed. "I poured out the deepest, darkest part of my soul to a man who was . . . very, very special to me, and then, five minutes later, I discovered that to him it was all in a day's work. I was hurt. I was *embarrassed*." She covered her still-red face with her hands. "I was angry with myself for my own stupidity. I haven't misread a man so completely since I was fifteen years old."

Adam had not spoken a word since she started her soliloquy, and suddenly Amy was certain that she didn't want him to. Anything he said could only make it worse. Quickly she started to babble, desperately trying to summon up a smile. "So how many brownie points do I get for all this honesty at the break of day, Dr. Reed? Enough to get you to take my place next time Timber Wolf draws K.P. duty?"

Finally he looked at her, his eyes dark and ineffably sad. "Amy—"

"Please, Adam. You don't have to say anything. In fact I'd rather you didn't. I'll be okay."

"Amy—"

"I know we're still friends. I'm kind of glad we got it out in the—"

"*Amy!!!*" This time his tone refuted all resistance. The hands that were jammed like iron into his pockets crawled, almost against his will, up to her shoulders until they lost themselves in her hair. He pressed her close enough to feel the buttons on his shirt; he rested his chin against the top of her head.

Amy's hands hung at her sides. She didn't know whether to hold him closer or push him away or cover her face and weep. It wasn't the kind of embrace he'd offered in the midst of her great confession, but it wasn't the kind that gave a forlorn lover new hope, either. Sorrow vibrated from every muscle in his tight, anguished body.

"I didn't want to say this, Amy; I thought it would be easier if I just kept dodging you." His voice was thick with pain. "But you've been far too brave for me not to tell you the truth."

He pulled back so she could see him, his hands still cupping her head. His eyes were as blue as the depths of the ocean as he spoke his next words. "You didn't misread me, honey. I tried to hide my feelings for you but I failed." He swallowed hard, then pushed the next words out like reluctant skyjumpers on their first time out. "I wanted you from the first minute we met. I still do. It gets worse every time we're together." His voice dropped to a whisper. "But there's nothing I can do about it, Amy. *Nothing*. Do you understand?"

Hope and hunger swirled in her heart. Instinctively she clung to his shirt. She didn't dare touch him, but she wasn't about to let him go. "No," she begged him. "I don't understand. Unless you're married or engaged or—"

"*NO.*"

She didn't know if he meant "No" to her question or "No" to her hope, but the anguished tone of his voice left any further protest stillborn.

He laid one palm against her cheek in a gesture that touched her more deeply than the most profound kiss she'd ever received from any other man. With a voice like shattered diamonds, he breathed, "Don't fight it, Amy; don't ask me to explain. Just be glad I told you once." He closed his eyes and dragged his hands from her face before he started down the trail. She could feel his pain as if it were her own as he whispered, "If you honor me, you'll let it be."

CHAPTER 8

LOOKING BACK Amy would never understand how she managed to get through morning watch with Adam sitting less than three feet away. She heard her own voice render a stirring version of "When Morning Gilds the Sky" and marveled that the singer did not dissolve into tears. She heard the pastor of Camp Colina pray for all of them, and wondered how he was able to speak at all. And when it was over—when the reprieve of breakfast came, during which she would sit as far away from this man as she possibly could—she saw the Pied Piper lead a band of children toward the lodge singing "Lord I Want to Be a Christian." Amy's fingers were numb as she plucked the guitar strings. She'd never felt less like a Christian in her life.

If you honor me, you'll let it be. What final, cruel, irrevocable words he'd uttered! How could she fight them? If she left him alone, she'd lose him for good . . . if she pressed him further, she would violate his trust. Her only comfort was the knowledge that he shared the anguish she was feeling; yet she knew that she would have borne any pain to prevent Adam's suffering.

I am in love with this man, she admitted to herself in the dark silence of her mind. *I promised him I'd stay here for seven days . . . I promised Joey and I promised Tiffany. This is one time I can't run away.*

"Are you all right?" Trevor suddenly asked from a spot near her elbows, sounding genuinely sympathetic. "You seem a little out of it this morning."

She didn't look at him, afraid he could read the precise cause of her anguish just by looking at her face. "Some days are better than others," she tossed out.

"Isn't that the truth." His eyes wandered off to Tiffany, who was doing her best to ignore Julie Ann's cheerful breakfast prattle. "My daughter still won't talk to me and Adam's decided that after today I'm flying solo in the Bible class." He shook his head. "As far as I can tell, this whole week is turning into a disaster."

And isn't that the truth, she wanted to weep. Instead she forced herself to study Trevor, who was, incredibly, wearing an old pair of jeans and a practical navy blue sweat shirt. "And here I was beginning to think you were starting to fit in," Amy managed to say. "At least you're learning to dress the part."

He glanced down at his expedient attire and forced a thin laugh. "I'm getting the hang of it. My wardrobe just couldn't endure any more of my Beau Brummel pride."

"Most of us could do with less pride, Trevor," Amy told him. "There are some things we just can't change. The sooner we accept them the better."

"You sound like you've been talking to Adam."

Actually, Amy thought she was talking *about* Adam, but she wasn't going to share that with Trevor. "Frankly, Trevor, I think we all could gain from taking a page out of Adam's book. He knows who he is and what he wants out of life. He never doubts that God is in his corner.''

So why can't he love me? What's his secret? What is it that's tearing him apart?

Before she could ponder her own question, Joey and a band of followers bounded up the trail with a riddle that Amy and the Giraffe simply *had* to guess. Then Pillsie and one of the counselors strolled by, wishing the two of them a sunny good morning. By the time that brief conversation was over, Amy was sure her moment of confidence with Trevor had ended, too.

But Trevor was resting both elbows on the table, still digesting her words. "How do you suppose he does it?'' he asked pensively.

"Does what?''

"Stays so up all the time. Always has a cheerful word for everybody. Turns every frown into a smile. He never gets angry . . . never feels hurt. . . .'' He stopped at the sight of Amy's blurred expression. "Do you know something I don't know?''

"He worries about us,'' Amy muttered quickly, eager to cover her blunder. "He's so determined to do the Lord's work here, to take care of the kids and the counselors. I think that's quite a burden on a man of his high standards. If he fell short of any of the goals he's set for himself this summer, I think he'd take it pretty hard.''

Trevor nodded in agreement, but nonetheless asked her, "You don't really think he's in danger of failing in some way, do you?''

Amy closed her eyes. "Not if you and I make it back to the Lord.''

"I didn't come here to find God, kiddo,'' Trevor retorted sharply. "I came here to set the stage for reclaiming my daughter. Now if Adam helps me with that—''

"Be honest with yourself, Trevor!'' Amy burst out.

"Why do you think you picked this place? There must be a thousand other ways you and Tiffy could have spent the summer! Just because you're fighting with the Lord doesn't mean you don't want to make up!"

He didn't answer right away. His brown eyes grew solemn as he studied his fingernails. "I take it you speak from . . . personal experience."

Amy nodded.

"Having . . . decided what my problem is, I suppose you have a solution?"

"Not exactly, but I do have a suggestion."

Slowly he turned to face her. She'd expected some stiff resistance, but Trevor surprised her.

"I'm listening."

She felt as though she were treading her way through a land mine, but she managed to find some words. "I think you and Tiffany—together or separately—should get some professional counseling. As luck would have it, you've got an expert in the field who's near at hand already praying for you. I think you'd be wise to take advantage of Adam's skill and compassion while you're here. After that . . . well, maybe he can recommend something . . . or someone."

Trevor didn't answer for a while. Amy knew this discussion wasn't easy for him, and no reply he'd have made would have surprised her. "You mentioned that . . . you had some troubles of your own to sort through. Are you up to taking your own advice?"

"You mean have I talked to Adam?"

He nodded.

"Yes. It helped a lot."

It was not until this moment that she realized what great strides in her grief she'd made because of Adam. Despite her anguish over the perplexing glitch in their relationship, his compassion had set her on the road to healing, and her guilt had lessened perceptibly since her dawn confession.

"He's a remarkably sympathetic listener, Trevor," she told him honestly. "He won't upbraid you for your shortcomings."

"What makes you think I have any shortcomings?"

At first Amy thought he was kidding, but then his tone gave way to bitter irony.

"Just because my daughter blames me for my wife's death and even God won't have anything to do with me?"

Forcing herself to rise above her own pain, Amy took his hand and squeezed it gently. "I'm not exactly on the Lord's good side right now either, Trevor, but I'll make you a deal. If I ever learn how to pray again, I'll pray for you. Will you do the same for me?"

For the first time she felt kinship with this man; she really understood that his macho bravado was a shield for the deepest kind of pain. He looked almost fearful as he whispered, "We better get on the stick and learn how, Amy, because it looks to me like we're both standing in the need of prayer."

A few tears trailed down Amy's face as he hugged her, but just for a second a fraction of the pain seemed to ebb. And then she stood up to return her plate and met Adam's anguished eyes, riveted upon her.

He stood at least thirty yards away. Half a dozen camp tables and at least fifty youngsters sat strung out between them, yet he seemed close enough to touch. For just a second his eyes slipped down to Trevor, then back to Amy's face. Without a word he turned and walked away.

The day went downhill from there on. The parable for the Bible study group was the one about the mustard seed and should have spoken to Amy's slowly blossoming faith. But Adam's defection had temporarily anesthetized all of her feelings—including her love for the Lord. She conducted the group in a somnambulent state; she couldn't even respond to the children's impromptu plans for role-playing the new parable during the evening service. She barely noticed that Julie Ann was sitting next to Tiffany, making every effort to include her in the discussion even though the blond girl remained stonily silent, her eyes on Amy's face.

Her expression remained the same throughout the morning's camp maintenance assignment—cleaning the lodge this time—and Amy's unsmiling lunch. She and Julie Ann followed Amy to the afternoon music group, where Julie Ann sang and Tiffany frowned for an hour. The children had gotten word of Adam's plans for Holy Communion later in the week and asked Amy to teach them a song for the event. With aching reluctance, she taught them "Let Us Break Bread Together on Our Knees." She even managed to talk a bit about the meaning of Communion and the essence of the Last Supper. But even as she spoke it occurred to Amy that if she were busy directing the children's choir, maybe nobody would bother to offer her Communion. Maybe she could avoid the entire experience. . . .

It wasn't the only thing she wanted to avoid. The chapel above the Jordan, Adam's morning trail, his office in the lodge; worship beside him, worship without him; days of hurt while she worked on his team, nights of emptiness while she pondered his words. . . .

It was late afternoon before Amy found the privacy that had eluded her all day. She edged up on the hill behind the bowl, out of sight of the pool and an unlikely place to run into Adam. But she was still haunted by the tone of his voice and the touch of his hands as he'd begged her to leave him alone. He couldn't be married, could he? Surely she'd have known! But then again, she hadn't known he was a minister either, and everybody else in the camp had taken that for a given. Why else would he be so adamant that he must stay away from her?

Once again she tried to look at things from his point of view. He was, after all, a man of great integrity . . . a man who would have been a man of God whether he sold stock or flew jets or collected garbage for a living. She couldn't help but wonder if things might have been different if they'd met somewhere else. And yet—he didn't seem interested in alternatives. He was adamant that there was absolutely no hope for anything between them.

"Howdy," Pillsie's crusty voice suddenly interrupted her reverie. "Kind of a lazy afternoon, isn't it?"

Amy looked up and tried to smile. She hadn't expected to run into anyone out here. In fact, she'd deliberately tried to choose an inconspicuous hiding place. "Yes, I guess it is."

"I reckon that's why you're sitting out here all alone in the sun when there's half a dozen good shade trees a stone's throw away?"

"Well, actually . . . I guess I didn't really notice," she replied with some embarrassment.

"Amy Shelby, you haven't noticed one single thing since dawn this morning. You came up here Sunday with a tiny burr in your saddle but now you've got a whole cactus stuck under the cinch. If your mama were here, I know she'd want you to tell it to somebody. Will I do?"

Amy didn't know whether to be touched or embarrassed. She'd been surprised that Pillsie even remembered her after all these years, and more surprised that she still cared so deeply for her mother. Yet she'd clearly been watching Amy since breakfast and cared enough to follow her out to this quiet patch of sun. It was the sort of thing Adam might do. Or assign someone else to do. . . .

"Did Adam send you up here?" she asked with some suspicion.

"Ha! Adam hasn't noticed I'm alive today. He's in

even worse shape than you are." Her eyes narrowed, shrewdly putting two and two together. "Would it be smarter to forget I said that?"

Amy met the older woman's eyes and desperately hoped for her cooperation. She worked very closely with Adam and was trusted by the entire staff. She probably already knew that they'd taken a hike together this morning. For Amy to pretend otherwise would sound more suspicious than the simple truth.

Struggling for words that would not damage this marvelous man who had crushed her at dawn, Amy said simply, "I'm having a rough time up here, Pillsie, working through some of my old feelings about . . . God and my mother. Adam's trying to help me, and sometimes we both get pretty frustrated that I'm so resistant to the Lord. There are times when I think I'll never be whole again, and times when he feels like he's . . . failing to save a lost sheep."

Pillsie squeezed Amy's hand in silent acceptance of her suffering, her eyes revealing both her knowledge of the deeper truth beyond the younger woman's words and her promise to keep that truth to herself.

"Adam Reed is one young minister I wouldn't fight, Amy," Pillsie told her with a gentle smile. "If he's taken on the task of helping you return to the Lord, I don't think you stand a chance of leaving Camp Colina until you've made your peace with Jesus."

In spite of everything, Amy couldn't help but agree.

It was almost swimming time before Amy left Pillsie to join the Timber Wolf girls under the giant cypress just south of the pool. Most of them were busy weaving plastic cord into what could have been dog leashes or necklaces. Amy's childhood recollection of this kind of macrame was that the end product was irrelevant. Everybody kept track of whose braid was the longest, period. You never needed to finish the project, and once you got home, it sat on a shelf for a month before your mother threw it out. But here at Colina, it was worth gold for a week.

"I just can't do this, Amos," Julie Ann complained, dumping her mangled green and blue cords on the grass. "It's hopeless."

"Nothing's hopeless," Amy reminded her, picking up the mess. "Some things just take a little more time than others."

Out of the corner of her eye she noticed that Tiffany was heading toward them. Predictably, she had waited until all the other girls had left the cabin before hiking down alone. But at least she was wearing her swimming suit. To Amy's surprise she carried a nest of plastic cords that had already been neatly plaited. It was the first camp activity she seemed to have undertaken by herself.

"Hi, Tiff," Amy greeted her warmly. "Hot enough for swimming, do you think?"

Tiffany shrugged. "There's nothing else to do."

The dour reference to swimming was not lost on Julie Ann. "Don't you like to swim, Tiffany? All my life I've wanted to, but I really don't know how."

The hostile youngster tossed her a disparaging look. "It's easy."

"Really?" the other girl repeated in wonder. "Could you teach me?"

Tiffany frowned. "I don't know. I didn't come up here to—"

"Don't worry about it, Julie Ann," Amy interrupted with a searing glance at Tiffany. "If Tiffy doesn't swim well enough to help you I'm sure that—"

"I swim real good!" Tiffany interjected. Her eyes dared Amy to deny it. "I like to do outdoor stuff."

"Well, that's great, Tiff!" she tossed out without meeting the girl's eyes. "Now you've got a swim coach, Julie Ann. Tiff'll have you dogpaddling in no time."

She handed Julie Ann the cord and tried to keep

131

from smiling in Tiffany's presence. She was sure that the girl knew she'd been manipulated, but for some reason this time she had allowed it to happen. Maybe even welcomed it.

"It looks so much better when you do it, Amos," Julie Ann sighed over the dog leash. "I'll never learn how."

"It's easy," Tiffany said again, taking Julie Ann's project with deft, sure hands. "It's like you're clapping out a song. Red one, blue one, green-and-white. Red one, blue one, green-and-white. Red one, blue one. . . ."

This time Amy turned away without a word. *Maybe this day won't be a total loss after all,* she consoled herself. *Even though God has given up on me, He still must believe in children.*

It was after five when the lifeguard cleared the children out of the pool. It was, of course, their regular time for a camp staff meeting; but there was no sign of Adam. Amy hadn't seen him since lunch.

"Go on, Joey," Trevor called to the little boy who was still practicing noisy half-dives off the side of the pool. "Hold a spot for me at dinner."

Amy grinned at her little brother and blew him a kiss, then waited while Trevor floated to her side. "Where's the boss?" he asked wryly.

"Adam?" Amy asked, feeling unaccountable awkward. "I have no idea."

"Well, it looks to me like the natives are getting restless. I think you better go ahead and start the meeting."

"Me?" Amy squawked, more alarmed by Trevor's reasons for perceiving her as next in command than by the possibility of taking over in Adam's absence. "Why do you think—"

'You're the church organist, aren't you?"

"Of course not. Kay is the—" She stopped as she

got his point. *Most of these people already consider you my assistant*, Adam had told her at dawn. More than once he'd dropped hints that he really needed her support to make this week a success. For some strange reason it was Amy, the prodigal, whom he seemed to trust the most. She couldn't imagine what emergency could be keeping Adam from fulfilling his obilgation, but she also had to doubt that anything she could do to cover his absence would be welcome.

"Well, gather around folks, and let's see what we need to discuss," she heard herself say, stifling a sigh of relief when Grand Slam and Pinky and the others instantly did as she asked without comment. Like Trevor, they seemed to take it for granted that she should be the one to fill in for Adam. "How did the new parable go?"

"Great," was the conglomerate message. All the children were eager for more role playing.

"Any concerns? Too much music? K.P. duty? Coyote serenades at night?"

"I like the coyotes," Pinky declared. "We live in the city. That's the one sound that let's me know I am *definitely* in the woods." She turned to Amy. "Have we reached any consensus about Holy Communion?"

Amy shook her head. "Some of the kids asked me about it. I taught them a song and we talked a little bit about what it means."

"I think we should have it the last night," Trevor suggested, causing Amy to think of Judas. "I think the 'last night' and 'remembrance' might have some meaning for them even if the body and blood of Christ are a bit beyond their comprehension."

"I don't know," she stalled. "It seems to me—"

"Let's take a vote," Grand Slam suggested. "I know Adam wants to have Communion, so we don't need to worry about countermanding him. How does everybody else feel?"

Amy shrank wordlessly into the water. There was

no artful way out of this. Aside from her own desire not to look like an idiot, she didn't want to let Adam down. He'd want her to keep the group together, uplifted, inspired.

The vote was unanimous. Amy, as erstwhile leader, had an excuse to abstain. Communion was scheduled for Friday night, pending Adam's final approval, which no one doubted would be forthcoming. Amy tossed out the idea of a group hike to Persistence Peak, and several people expressed interest. They spent a few more minutes discussing minor points of camp life and praising everybody's efforts. And then, quite suddenly, there was nothing left to talk about. It was time for a closing prayer.

Amy froze, certain that this was one assignment she could not complete. She looked at each face, gathered hand in hand as though they ringed a dinner table, and wondered if words would come to her lips. The words that came belonged to her mother, who had always said grace or delegated the honor to someone of her choosing.

"Pinky," Amy whispered, choosing a certain ally, "Would you like to lead us in prayer this afternoon?"

Without missing a beat the Christian woman spoke to Jesus for the group, expressing in words all the things that Amy wished she could have said. She thanked the Lord for the majesty of the pines, the warmth of the children, the unimpeachable spiritual guidance of Adam Reed. She thanked Him for all the children and counselors who were making the week so special, and especially for Amos Shelby who was proving so worthy of her Biblical name. She prayed that the decision to offer Holy Communion to the children who were baptized was not premature, and that all those who witnessed the Gift of Salvation would be uplifted by it. She had just joined in the communal "Amen" when Adam appeared on the trail.

He was still dressed in the jeans and tee-shirt he'd worn that morning, and he looked like he'd hardly stopped all day. His sandy hair was dusty and coated with tiny leaves and dried grass. Half a dozen people greeted him as they dispersed for dinner. It was some time before he could make his way to Amy.

But there was no doubt that she was the destination at the end of his path. He headed directly toward her, his eyes dark and full of the same nameless understanding that had bound them together before their strange parting at dawn. Amy's breath began to quicken as he approached her. Suddenly she wished that Trevor were not standing by her side.

"I hear you had to take over the meeting for me," Adam told her, his eyes full of gratitude and pride. "I also heard you did a really good job. I guess I picked the right prophet as your namesake."

Suddenly Amy remembered who that prophet was. The shepherd who was certain he couldn't possibly preach the Word and fought with Lord tooth and toenail in his desire to be left alone. But when push came to shove, Amos had done just fine! He'd fulfilled every one of God's expectations for him.

The pleasure on Adam's face—after her own day of unextinguished pain—suddenly filled Amy with anger. "You did that on purpose! How dare you! You're not the Lord and you have no right to manipulate my faith even if you *are* a pastor!"

"Amy!" He looked shocked. "Not for a minute did I—"

"For your information, I had Pinky say the blessing so you didn't win after all. I—"

"I had an emergency, Amy! I couldn't have come to the meeting no matter what!" His sincerity was undeniable. "I knew you'd take over and that relieved my mind, but I swear to you, Amy, I had no choice."

"Take it easy, Amy," Trevor interjected, speaking for the first time. "I don't know what's going on here, but—"

"What was your emergency?" Amy knew she was yelling at Adam for all the wrong reasons, but the pain was so great she had to lash out. She didn't even acknowledge Trevor's presence, and neither did Adam. "What could possibly be so vital?"

For a long time Adam said nothing, weighing his options. She knew that another man would have lied to her; whatever it was he'd been doing, he clearly did not want her to know. When at last he spoke, his voice was weary and still laced with stress.

"One of Grand Slam's kids spotted a rattler in the meadow while they were playing ball. It slithered under Timber Wolf Cabin before anybody could reach it. It's taken me all afternoon to get it out."

The blood drained from Amy's face. She knew that both men would think she was afraid for herself, but a different concern blocked her thoughts. Visions of venomous fangs thundering into Adam's body filled her mind and paralyzed her heart. Her anger was swallowed up by the depth of her fear. "Are you all right?" she whispered. "It didn't—"

He shook his head, reaching out just once to squeeze her clammy fingers. "Everything's fine. Nobody got hurt." He paused, the late afternoon sun leaving his face in unreadable shadows. Gently he released her from his grasp. "It's all over now."

And that, Amy concluded, was really the bottom line. She could already feel the shutters moving back into place between them. Trevor, however, had more to say.

"You mean there are *rattlers* in this camp? You just let them wander around loose? Under Timber Wolf Cabin?"

Adam tried to calm the other man. "I'm told it's very rare they come right into camp, Trevor. As long as everybody wears hiking boots on the trails and keeps their eyes open, there usually is not any problem." The dinner bell rang to punctuate his last statement, reminding Amy that she was standing in a dripping swimming suit that was *still* the wrong size, the wrong color . . . and made her look like a mud hen.

"I'm going to go check," Trevor declared brusquely. "I don't like this at all. Come on, Amy."

Amy stalled for just a minute as Trevor reached for his towel and started up the rise. Adam's eyes were dark and cautious as he trailed the other man for several feet, then swept back to caress Amy.

A tight band of restraint gripped the muscles of Adam's face as he tried to sound casual. "I knew I could count on you, Amy. I knew you wouldn't let me down . . . in spite of everything."

I love you, Adam Reed, she wanted to say. *We are partners, just as you always wanted us to be. In spite of everything. . . .*

Instead she struggled for complacent words that would not embarrass either of them. "I'm glad I could help out, Adam. Now if you'll excuse me, I think I better catch up with Trevor."

"There's really no reason for him to be upset," Adam declared abruptly, his voice masking the tiniest hint of a tremble. "The Lord has placed all of you in my care, and I have no intention of letting Him down."

"It's not that Trevor doesn't trust you, Adam," Amy managed to say, wondering if his sudden prickliness was due to Trevor's actions or some other cause. "But there's somebody in Timber Wolf Cabin who's very precious to him and he just doesn't want anything to happen to her."

Adam's eyes swept over Amy one more time, silent and veiled. He could have been referring to any one of the girls in Timber Wolf Cabin—or to their black-maned counselor—when he whispered in a strained and husky tone, "Believe me, Amy, I know just how Trevor feels."

137

CHAPTER 9

THE NEXT DAY WAS A REPEAT of the one before, except that everything at Camp Colina got a little better, a little warmer, a little easier for Amy. She had stopped waiting for Adam.

She hadn't stopped hurting, of course, and she hadn't stopped wondering what stringent belief forced him to deny her love. But she knew that Pillsie was right; he was a man of powerful integrity. And somehow, since he felt as strongly about their separation as he did, she would have been a little disappointed in him if he'd changed his mind.

Ironically, now that he'd stopped dogging her footsteps, goading her to read the Bible and find the Lord, Amy felt compelled to intensify that search on her own. She was tempted to borrow Joey's Bible in the hopes that she might have better luck opening one that didn't belong to Adam. But the memory of his eyes the first night he'd prayed for her stilled her tongue. She would read Adam's Bible before she left this camp. Somehow, she was certain, the Lord would make it happen.

There were times at camp when she was filled with the music, the scent of pine, that special knowledge that He was near. Her morning walk took a different direction—as far away from Adam's regular trail as possible—but she gained strength from his voice at morning watch, in prayer and in praise. Somehow they managed to work together, sing together, plan music and worship and discuss hurting kids. Not once since the rattler incident did his eyes beg hers for understanding; never did his tone hint at anything but pastoral concern. He was guarded with her, and the special closeness they'd once shared seemed to be a thing of the past. But they were both working incredibly hard at making things easier for each other, and Amy struggled to take comfort from that.

On Wednesday afternoon, Grand Slam and Pinky challenged Grizzly and Timber Wolf to a baseball game. It wasn't really a fair match, since Grand Slam had been training most of his kids all week and Amy, who was only moderately interested in sports, could out-hit, out-catch, and out-pitch Trevor with one hand tied behind her back! But the kids were enthusiastic about the challenge, so she decided to have some fun. Anything would be better than spending the afternoon sitting under a tree mourning the loss of Adam.

The game started simply enough. The diamond had almost no boundaries and each team had over a dozen players. The counselors pitched, the kids squealed and nobody played much baseball. It wasn't until the fifth inning that Tiffany, who had been watching rather blandly from her spot just off first base, called out to Trevor, "I think you should let me pitch, Dad."

At the time Trevor was heading toward the mound, despite his disastrous performance the inning before. Amy wasn't at all sure how he'd respond to his daughter's request. In a sense she was insinuating that he was a lousy pitcher—which was undiplomatic but certainly true. On the other hand, it was the first time she'd voluntarily spoken to him since they'd arrived, let alone voiced a strong preference for *anything*. Whether or not she even got the ball remotely close to the plate was, in Amy's view, irrelevant.

"Can she do that, Amy?" Joey called out from his spot in left field. "I thought only counselors could pitch."

It occurred to Amy with some delight that it was the first time Joey had spoken to her since the game began. He'd been just as friendly and affectionate as ever the last two days, but his focus was becoming more and more his peers at Camp Colina and less and less on his human pacifier from home. And all in all, she had to admit with sisterly pride, he didn't really play ball much worse than any of the other kids.

"You're on, Tiff," Trevor announced with a thoughtful glance at his daughter. He tossed her the ball as she took over the mound, then called out to no one in particular, "I taught her everything she knows."

The first pitch to Nathan went straight up in the air, and everybody laughed. Except for Tiffany. The second ball sailed half way up to the slope to the lodge, and the catcher was gone almost three full minutes trying to retrieve it. Tiffany's small body grew tight as she stood defiantly on the mound. For a second Amy was afraid she was going to give up altogether. She didn't look like a tough tomboy any more; she looked like a little girl who'd bitten off way more than she could chew.

And then Julie Ann, who had opted to root from the sidelines rather than risk failure at this "boy's game," called out, "Come on, Tiffy! I know you can do it! Nobody's better than you!"

The next pitch was a strike in anybody's book. Tiffany looked like she'd pitched the last out in the World Series! Pride fairly glistened from her fair features. She pitched again and again, striking out the batter even by Camp Colina's very generous standards. Slowly, from the inside out, she began to glow.

For a seven-year-old her skills were mediocre. Any serious Little League player could have shredded her pride. But at Camp Colina, where the magic of love and the spirit of Jesus reigned over every nook and cranny of hillside, every scrawny pine tree and every tiny camper, she was declared the day's heroine solely by virtue of being able to pitch almost hittable strikes.

She wore out after three innings, of course, but it didn't matter in the least. An honest to goodness childhood grin had etched itself on her face, and grumpy, sour-faced Tiffany Grant just couldn't seem to wipe it off. In fact, a shrewd observer might have guessed that the old Tiffany Grant had just disappeared altogether.

"Please tell me I did something right this time, Amy," Trevor pleaded an hour later as the two of them lounged under a nest of pines near the empty ballfield. "I *did* play catch with her when she was little."

Amy grinned. "You earned yourself half a dozen brownie points today, Trev. And Tiffany won a Gold Medal."

He laughed. "She was always pretty athletic. Always wanted to help me outside. You know, pulling out all the weeds I missed—"

"You mean the ones behind you left for her?"

"No—I mean the seedlings!" Again he laughed. "Of course she was only three then. It was sort of hard to explain to her. Funny," he mused thoughtfully, "she doesn't seem to remember that. She thinks her mother did all the yardwork."

Amy sat up straighter, tucking her knees under her chin. "How long . . . if it's okay to ask this . . . how long have you been gone, Trevor?"

141

He sighed heavily and tugged a huge clump of pine needles out of the ground. "Almost two years, Amy."

Amy was stunned. "You never saw her . . . called her . . . wrote to her in all that time?"

He shrugged. "I felt like she was in an armed camp. Her grandmother hated me, and on the few occasions I saw Tiff right after her mother died, she made it pretty clear she hated me, too."

"Trevor, she was only a little girl!"

"I know. I know!" Pain filled his voice. "But I felt so guilty; don't you see? I'd been neglecting both of them—Tiffany and Carolyn—for quite a while before Carolyn died. The marriage had gone sour, and I'd taken on an extra project at work. . . ." He turned angry eyes on Amy's frankly disbelieving stare. "It's the truth, Amy! I won't admit I hadn't started thinking about other women, but I hadn't . . . I hadn't done anything about it yet."

"But you would have," Amy concluded softly, knowing this lay at the heart of his guilt.

After a long silence, he whispered, "Yes. I probably would have."

For several minutes neither of them spoke. Finally it was Amy who said, "You know I lost my mother, don't you, Trevor?"

He nodded. "I heard you mention it to Tiff. I asked Adam to tell me more about it, but he wouldn't say a thing."

A tiny part of Amy's heart smiled at that piece of news. She was right to trust Adam Reed. Even though she couldn't have him, she would leave here knowing that at least one decent, honorable man did exist in the world, and she would always love him.

"I'm not sure I want to tell you a lot about it, either, Trevor, except that . . . I know a lot about how guilt can eat away at a person, eat away at a family, year after year. It doesn't get any better. It won't go away by itself. Sooner or later, you've got to ask God

142

to forgive you and go on living. For Tiffy's sake, if not for your own."

Trevor watched her closely. "I presume you're still speaking from experience?"

She nodded.

"And you . . . have asked God for this forgiveness? And received it?"

How she wished she could have told him yes! But the best she could manage was a hoarse confession. "I've tried, Trevor. I'm still trying. But one thing I've learned up here—one thing that Adam's taught me—is that the problem isn't that God's not ready to listen. It's that I'm not ready to be forgiven. I'm not done whipping myself."

For several minutes Trevor did not speak. At last he reached out for Amy's hand, drawing strength from her efforts at self-healing.

"She had just started kindergarten when I left. I didn't think I could raise a little girl by myself. I still don't think it's going to be easy. But the time finally came when I knew I just couldn't go on pretending I didn't have a daughter. I'd have to face the fire-breathing dragon—Carolyn's mother—and reclaim my child."

Amy squeezed his hand, knowing how desperately he needed her support. "Are there . . . legal complications now? Will she try to get custody of Tiffy on the grounds that you abandoned her?"

He shook his head. "I don't know. I think it depends on Tiff. If she can convince her grandmother that she really wants to live with me, I think she'll let her go. But for months the two of them have been dissecting my flaws, blaming me for everything that ever went wrong. . . ." He sighed heavily. "I doubt that Tiffany can even remember the truth anymore. She was so young."

"She's still pretty young, Trevor," Amy reminded him. "She's still a little girl who needs her daddy more than anything else in the whole world."

Trevor managed to smile. He released Amy's hand and brushed one hand across his eyes. "And you, Miss Shelby? Are you still a little girl who needs her daddy?"

"No. . .," she answered slowly, pondering the question as Bill Shelby's round, loving face appeared before her eyes. "But I am a young woman who still loves her father very much. And in a sense, I'm the one who abandoned him."

Trevor met her eyes directly. "Then I guess it's time for you to go back home."

She nodded as the pieces fell in place. "It's time for me to accept what is. My father managed it a long time ago."

They shared a special smile before Trevor announced, "This is going to sound kind of strange, Amy, but I think I'm really glad you didn't fall for me. You've given me so much this week as a friend, and I know I never could have opened up to you this way if we'd been . . . well, romantically involved."

Instantly she thought of Adam and her tearful confession before she knew the truth about his life. She'd been able to share her feelings with him precisely because there were so terribly close; but Trevor was a different kind of person, and she knew he would not have risked his ego with a woman he was still trying to impress.

Her thoughts, embracing Adam, drifted back to the mountainside where he'd poured out his pain, and she wondered for the hundredth time why it was that he could not love her. Had he made that decision before her confession? Or was it that . . . once he knew the truth of her past . . . he really couldn't be quite as forgiving as he wanted to be?

Out of nowhere Trevor's voice jolted her back into reality. "You're in love with him, aren't you, Amy?"

She did not look up; she did not confirm his words or deny them.

"At first I was sure he felt the same way," he continued in a soothing tone. "Now I guess . . . oh, I don't know, Amy . . . I guess I'm just trying to say I'm sorry. I wish it could have worked out differently for you."

"So do I, Trevor," she confessed, feeling the agony all over again. "So do I."

With a friend's loving care, Trevor put both arms around her and let Amy shed the tears she'd kept locked up for the last two days. Neither one of them noticed the tall, blond man watching them from the far side of the Jordan River. Neither one of them saw the look of anguish on his face as he began to pray.

"Amy's been telling me about the hike to Persistence Peak that she took every year as a kid, Adam," Trevor announced that evening as the three of them ambled back toward the meadow after worship at the bowl. Ever since their afternoon chat he'd been exceptionally solicitous, and Amy knew he was talking more to protect her from an awkward silence with Adam than for any other reason. "We thought Friday would be the best day to do it, since the Bible study will mainly be review."

Adam did not respond at first. He looked not at Trevor, but at Amy; his words were still, dropped like pebbles into a stream.

"Who's 'we'? Just the two of you?"

"Well . . . yes," Trevor answered. "Originally we thought there would be another cabin or two joining us, but now it looks like—"

"Are you taking all of the kids in your Bible classes along?"

"Well . . . we could, I guess," Trevor hedged, obviously taken aback by Adam's inquisition. "But since there's two of our kids in every group, and between us we've got two cabins, that's eight kids who wouldn't be there and only twelve, altogether, if somebody filled in for each of us—"

"Somebody?" Again he looked at Amy. No, he *glared* at Amy. "Whom did you have in mind?"

She refused to answer; this was Trevor's conversation. But Trevor was already in quicksand. He'd never seen Adam harsh about anything, and his resistance to this group hike didn't seem to make any sense.

"Well . . . you seem to be free in the mornings, Adam," he finally tossed out.

"I already know how to teach the parables."

"Well . . . that's just the point."

"Yes, it is . . . isn't it?"

Adam knew that Trevor didn't understand, but she certainly did. Adam wasn't worried about the kids missing Bible class, or his role in filling in. He thought they were both running away from an experience they needed . . . or at the very least just running away to frolic.

"It's only one day, Adam," she finally offered in Trevor's defense. "Besides, we'll need to take a rest break on the trail and we could discuss Friday's parable with them. The week just wouldn't seem complete to me without this hike. We did it every year."

"Then maybe you should go by yourself after camp is over." His eyes darkened. "Or you could go together after the kids are gone, seeing that you have so much in common."

"What's that supposed to mean?" Amy demanded.

"It means I think you ought to weigh your priorities." His voice was tight. "Figure out what you want out of this week and whether it's fair to the kids to decide what they want when they're too young to understand your motivation."

This time his meaning was crystal clear, and Amy's face went into instant bloom. "Stow your insinuations, Adam Reed," she ground out fiercely, oblivious to the surprise that gilded Trevor's face. "Nobody at

Camp Colina is supposed to hike out of hollering distance alone and you know it. Family groups traditionally do this sort of thing together! Besides, his daughter is in my cabin and my brother is in his. On top of that—"

"Amy, cool down!" Trevor begged her. "You don't want to yell at him like that."

"Why not?" she thundered, knowing perfectly well that Trevor was only trying to save her from her own folly.

"Well—" Clearly Trevor was stuck for an answer that would stop her tirade but not expose her heart to Adam. In desperation he sputtered, "Because he's a preacher."

He couldn't have said anything worse. Suddenly Adam was as angry as Amy. "What's that got to do with anything, Trevor?"

Simmering, Amy struggled for control. She couldn't let Trevor get dragged into this; he needed Adam too much to feel estranged because of her. She knew that her white-hot words had nothing to do with the Bible class or the hike, let alone the fact that Adam was a pastor. She also knew he'd rather have her honest fury than false white-washed courtesy in honor of his robe. But she couldn't bear his insinuations that she and Trevor were using the kids as an excuse to go off cavorting together. He knew better! He knew she wanted *him*, and he knew she'd started to watch over Trevor only because he'd asked her to.

She glared at both men, then chose her words with care. "I suppose I should apologize, *Doctor* Reed. But then again, I imagine you're old enough to know that any man who acts like a child can expect to be treated like one."

She was gratified by a full thirty seconds of Adam's speechless disbelief before she stalked away.

CHAPTER 10

IT WASN'T UNTIL AFTER BREAKFAST the next morning that Adam sought her out for a private moment. She was doing dishes with her girls and was still pretty irritated with him . . . and with herself. Her explosion the night before had been inevitable under the circumstances, but still she had to admit that Adam wasn't the only one who'd been out of line.

"Do you have a minute, Amy?" His conciliatory tone only heightened her remorse.

"I'm smart enough to listen and wash at the same time," she answered blandly, afraid to look at him.

"If I help you finish up, could you spare me a minute or two before class?"

She could hear the smile in his voice, that laughing, teasing sound that told the world he was in a playful mood. She could imagine the dimples that tugged at the edges of his enticing mouth. If things had been different between them, she could have responded in the same spirit of fun. But she was too depressed to play the game.

"Okay. But make it snappy. Yesterday I was a few

minutes late and total mayhem broke loose in the room.''

"You can say that again," Tiffany mumbled from somewhere on her left.

It was a surprise to hear Tiffany say anything. Of course, after yesterday's tiny miracle almost anything could happen. She found a smile for her young friend.

"Well, I'll be on time today, Tiff," she promised, trying to act as though conversation with the troubled girl were an everyday affair. "Today's parable is one of my favorites. It's about a man who didn't have enough courage to follow his own instincts and use his Godgiven talents. I always thought that was such a pity." She pondered the message for a moment, and then added bravely, "It would be sort of like somebody who can pitch like you refusing to play baseball.''

Tiffany stifled a smile and almost met her glance. "Or you deciding not to sing," she mumbled.

Adam, wrangling the dishtowel beside Amy, took a deep breath. Their eyes met; then she forced herself to say, "Yes, Tiffany. That's what it would be like.''

"I guess you can go late to class, Amos, if your assistant will fill in," Adam commented, warming the young girl with a wink. "I think she got the point of the story a whole lot quicker than you did.''

Amy was about to hurl some grim retort in his direction when she noticed, incredibly, the tiniest hint of a smile on Tiffany's face. Adam noticed it too, and brave soul that he was, he reached out and grazed her cheek with a gentle hand. "You know," he commented thoughtfully, his eyes still holding Tiffany's, "I've always said that kids are a lot smarter than grownups. Something happens to people as they grow older. They stop eating carrots, or something.''

Tiffany laughed. It was only for a moment, but she actually laughed! Amy wanted to throw her arms around her, around Adam, praise God and go tell

149

Trevor, but she restrained herself. "I guess that'll do it, Adam. Follow me over here—I left my guitar on the table."

Wordlessly they sauntered out of the kitchen, taking great care not to speak until they were beyond Tiffany's line of vision.

"How did you do that?" Amy asked, truly impressed. "For days I've done everything but stand on my head—"

"Which is why I finally broke the ice. You've been melting the glacier—she was just ready to let the sunshine in. I suspect we're going to hear a lot more laughter coming from that child as long as we don't let on how excited we are."

Amy grinned. "Still, it makes my whole day." Quickly she told him about the ball game, then tacked on, "If I can get Tiffy to come to grips with herself—and her father—my whole trip here will be worthwhile."

His gaze narrowed. "And otherwise it won't be?"

She couldn't very well tell him that she'd not only lost her soul but her heart as well in the five short days since she'd come to this sacred place, so she whispered simply, "My time here isn't over yet. I'm sure there are a few more mysteries yet to be unraveled."

He studied her eyes for a minute, taking in the long lashes and sober gray depths, before he whispered, "I'm sorry about last night."

"So am I." She hadn't meant to give him any quarter, but the words had just spilled out without permission.

"There's really no good reason why you and Trevor shouldn't take that hike, Amy," he started off companionably, laying a hand on her shoulder. "The rattlers aren't any more prevalent than they've ever been, and I trust you enough not to be too concerned about propriety—"

"Propriety???"

150

"And I know you've got a lot in common with Trevor—"

"And what exactly is it that you think we have in common?" Amy demanded, turning away so sharply that she dislodged the fraternal arm slung so indifferently around her shoulders. "Are we both such pathetic heathen spectacles that we appear to you like bookends as you gaze down upon us from the lofty heights of your spiritual perfection?"

The words tumbled out, unplanned and unbridled; Amy was helpless to call them back even if she'd wanted to. Looking at Adam's face—bright with surprise and red with shame—she wasn't sure whether she wanted to or not. For an endless parade of guitar-string tight seconds he stared at her before he found his footing and looked away. Cautiously he straightened, brushing his short hair with nervous fingers.

"Amos . . . Amy. . . ." he started hesitantly, "I don't think I've . . . done a very good job conveying to you my . . . true feelings about this situation."

"What situation? We just want to take a day hike that's been standard for every batch of campers at Camp Colina for as long as anyone can remember. Just because *you've* never done it before doesn't mean that somebody else can't."

"I've talked to Orville about the trail since you first mentioned it Monday. Nobody's checked it out since the last rain. The part near his cabin is a mess, and he suspects the rest is even worse."

"Then give us some shovels and we'll clean it up. I'm not expecting to hike up a white shag carpet." Suddenly her eyes brimmed with tears. "You know I need to do it. You know I need to look for Him everywhere I ever found Him before. You promised to help me, Adam! But ever since you found out what I *really* did you've either ignored me or hassled me or just gotten in the way!"

Amy knew she was out of control, hurling words at him like spears in self-defense. For days she'd tried to stifle the agony within her. She'd worn a plastic smile like a good trooper; she'd backed him up in every instance where public trust demanded it. But suddenly her resistance had snapped. She just couldn't go on pretending that he hadn't crushed the very fiber of her being. She couldn't hold back the suspicions that still chased around in her head, even though she knew they were not worthy of the man. "What happened to your open ear, your insight, your wordless compassion? Did they all flee your robust faith when you discovered what a hideous sin I really committed?"

He looked just like she'd slapped him in the face; he even reeled from the blow. For an endless storm of black silence he said nothing. Then he reached out for her face with both hands, fingers tucked deep in her hair as his thumbs cupped each ear, and forced her to look at him.

"You are so wrong, Amy. I know I've treated you poorly—God knows I tried to do the best I could. But it just about killed me when I realized you had to stay here—"

"*Had* to stay!" Amy sputtered. "You begged me to stay! You practically forced me to! How dare you make it seem like I inflicted myself on you!"

"Amy!" It was almost a shout, even though he was just inches away from her face. She froze, not at all certain of her next move. His eyes were dark blue, electric blue, with none of the tender silence she'd grown to know. He was aroused with some emotion she had not seen in him before, and she could neither read it nor respond. Overwhelmed and even a little frightened, she dropped her eyes and waited for him to speak.

For several more moments only silence radiated between them. His hands seemed white-coal hot on her ears; she was sure his fingertips were trembling.

152

Yet when he released her, neither the fire nor the trembling seemed to go away. She glanced up, uncertain, but it was the back of Adam's head that faced her.

"I'm sorry, Amy. I never meant to hurt you. I never meant to hurt myself." He paused, gathering words as slowly as a child collects blackberries in a thorny patch. He shoved both hands deep in his pockets before his eyes skipped over hers uncertainly. "I am deeply gratified that you were able to share your trials with me, and I would be the last one to judge you for a wisp of unsteady judgment you may have committed as a child. I never expected you to take my . . . unavoidable comments about you and Trevor that way."

"How exactly did you expect me to take them? You've been making snide remarks about the two of us ever since . . . ever since. . . ." She stopped, unable to find words to describe that ineffable, life-changing morning they'd shared on the mountain. "Ever since I told you about my mother."

"Amy!" He threw his hands up in exasperation. "Are you so bound up in your own griefs that you can see none of mine? I'm trying so hard to be your pastor, but when I see you having fun with Trevor I can only respond as a man." For just a second he let his eyes underline his words. "I'm so jealous, Amy. I can hardly bear to look at him."

This time it was Amy who tucked her hands in her pockets. She honestly did not understand. *You had your chance. I all but threw myself at you and still you tossed me away.* Out loud she said, "I can't imagine why you would be jealous of Trevor. He's lost his wife; he's estranged from his daughter; he's hollow and empty and a little overweight and hasn't the vaguest idea how to become whole again. He's—"

"He's free to love you."

The words echoed through the quiet pines, circling

153

Amy's ears until they came to rest on the heavy silence of her chest. Somehow she found the courage to meet Adam's eyes, intensely blue with fear and desire that amazed her, frightened her . . . filled her with delirious new hope.

But before she could speak, a voice at the door of the lodge began to bellow, "Amos! Phone call for you!" Pillsie shouted the words in staccato phrases that might reach clear across the meadow, even though Amy stood less than fifty feet away. "Long distance!"

She had to glance at Pillsie; had to wave across the rustic dining tables to indicate she'd heard. Then she had to look back at Adam, knowing she had to leave him . . . knowing he might never allow himself to talk to her like this again.

"Better get a move on, Amos," he tossed out as casually as if she were one of the kids. "Give me your guitar. I'll drop it off at Timber Wolf for you."

She could only hope he'd wait a while to make that delivery . . . until she was back at the cabin. Alone.

"Hello? This is Amy Shelby."

"It's Kay, Amy. Is everything all right?"

There were, of course, any number of answers that she could have made to that inquiry, but she knew that for Kay only one piece of data was required. "Joey's fine. He was a little bit clingy at first, but now I hardly see him. He's just having a ball."

There was a great sigh of relief on the other end of the line. Amy could picture Kay, her short blond waves framing her pale, pretty face; her small, shapely figure perched on the stool in the kitchen. She was probably even biting her nails.

"He hasn't . . . gotten lost or anything?"

"How could he get lost? You know how close together everything is up here—"

"No, I don't, Amy. You forget that I've never been there."

154

Well I sure won't forget you're not here this time!
Amy thought resentfully, suddenly blaming Kay for
the pain of Adam's defection. "Well, there's always
next year."

To her surprise, Kay asked cautiously, "Is . . .
everything going all right for you, Amy?"

"Why wouldn't it be?"

Again there was a long pause. "Your father . . .
was very surprised . . . pleased and surprised . . . that
you so readily agreed to spend the week up there,
Amy. He couldn't believe that nobody had to talk you
into it."

"Oh, Kay!" Amy couldn't help it; she started to
laugh.

"Amy?"

"Oh, Kay!" she repeated. "You were so sick I'll
have to forgive you. But I've got to tell you that I
hadn't the slightest idea that you two intended for me
to take over for the whole week. Once I got up here
the camp director nailed my hide to the wall and I
couldn't escape. So tell Dad—"

"Oh, Amy, I'm so sorry!" There was no denying
her sincerity. "We never meant to back you into a
corner. We just—"

"It's okay. I'm really glad I came." Until the words
were out Amy didn't know she meant them. In spite
of the pain Adam had inflicted upon her, she wouldn't
have missed meeting him for anything in the world.
Furthermore, there was no denying that something
monumental was happening to her in this sacred
place—something that was part Adam, part Tiffany,
part Joey and part the Lord Himself—and it was
perfectly obvious, even to *her*, that Camp Colina was
precisely where she was destined to be this fine week
in early June.

"Are you sure, Amy? I had this dream. . . ." Her
voice trailed off.

"I can't hear you too well, Kay. This phone is
about forty years old. Can you speak up?"

155

"I said I had a dream. That's why I called. You were . . . crying. In some kind of darkness. There were no trees, no cabins, no lights. And you just kept sobbing, 'I can't find him. I can't find him,' over and over again. I was sure you meant Joey. Your father said it was just my maternal nerves, but I . . . I just had to call you anyway. I hope you don't mind."

Amy was quiet for a minute. She could have belittled Kay's fears or ignored them, and she knew perfectly well that a week ago she would have done exactly that. But Adam's face, stern and yet imbued with Light, seemed to loom before her, urging her to reach out across the wire.

"Kay . . . I've had some dark nights here. But it isn't Joey I'm looking for. It isn't Joey I've lost. We're closer now than we ever have been. I'm really learning to love my little brother."

"Oh, Amy!" The words flew out of Kay's mouth, and then she began to cry. "Praise God," she wept. "Oh, thank you, Lord. How I've prayed for this."

Amy didn't know quite what to say. She was moved and embarrassed and suddenly irritated by the indifference of the telephone. She had never wanted to touch Kay before, never wanted to search her face. Yet suddenly there were bonded by such simple, changeless facts! *I love her son. She prayed for me.*

"Kay . . . when we get back we need to sit down and talk. Really talk. I need to talk with Dad, too—"

"Oh, Amy!" She was still weeping. "Forgive me for blubbering so. If you only knew. If you only knew. . . ." She couldn't really seem to go on. Amy didn't know whether to hang up or try to share some of the week's astounding discoveries. How could she bottle them up over the phone? How could she explain her tumultuous soul to a woman she'd done her best to ignore—maybe even wound—for months?

"Kay . . . could you tell Dad . . . could you tell him that . . . I think everything's going to be okay now?

Tell him that I love him. Tell him that . . . I'll sit with him in church next Sunday. . . . ''

Kay broke down again, and Amy realized, with twenty-twenty hindsight, that Kay had known her secrets right from the start, as had her father. How many times the two of them must have prayed for her! How many ways had she wounded the familyness of their newfound love!

"How did this miracle happen, Amy? How is it that you're finding your way home after all this time?"

It wasn't really an easy question to answer, but Amy did her best. "Somebody . . . somebody very special saw deep inside my heart enough to know I needed a little bit of help. He got me pointed in the right direction and trusted Jesus to do the rest."

When Kay stopped weeping it was only to say, "Whoever he is . . . whoever that miracle worker is, you give him a hug for me, will you, Amy?"

"I will if I can, Kay," she whispered. *And one for myself as well.* Only when she faced the impossibility of that dream did Amy realize that she too was beginning to shed her first tears.

By the time Amy reached the Redwood Room, she was fifteen minutes late for Bible study. It wasn't intentional; she hadn't even remembered the class until she'd hung up the phone and dried her eyes. By then it was too late to speculate on whether or not Adam or Pillsie had noticed her dilemma and decided to fill in for her.

Yet as she approached the tiny room, the door was open, but no boisterous sounds reached her ears. Arms and legs clad in jeans and tee-shirts were clearly visible through the doorway, so obviously somebody was inside! Grateful and intrigued, Amy stood outside for just a moment, listening.

"So, I don't know if that way it's written in here is just like I told you," Tiffany's high pitched, nervous voice filtered out to the hall, "but that's the way my mom always told me this story. And the point of it all is that if you don't do nothing—if you don't take no chances—you don't never get nothing good. You just sit there and stay the same, and that's dumb. It's boring. So no matter what you think might happen, ya gotta go out there and do your best, like those guys in the Olympics or those missionaries who teach school without no books, or Amos coming up here without no clothes or no idea she was supposed to stay here and be a counselor and then turned out to be the best teacher in the place!"

Amy closed her eyes and uttered the nearest thing to a prayer of gratitude she'd managed to breathe in seven years.

"So now let's go ahead and try to read it in the book, just to see if I got it right. Do any of you guys know how to read real good?"

Amy had to clear her throat and dry her eyes all over again before she entered the room.

"You didn't really think I was going to let you get away with that, did you?" Hours had passed since their last private encounter, but Adam's final words were still etched in Amy's mind.

He was bending over the fire at the bowl, slowly stoking its lazy ashes into life. The smell of woodsmoke, which always lingered for hours after the evening service, clung to Amy's face and her clothes as she waited for an answer.

"Nope," he mumbled, not turning to face her, "I guess not."

She waited for him to continue but he said nothing. She studied her borrowed blue sweat shirt and wished she had something prettier—anything at all—to wear while he explained his inner torment. But Amy knew it was not her lack of elegant finery that kept this man from her side.

He's free to love you, he'd tossed out in agony. What did that mean? It didn't provide her any more information, but she couldn't help but pretend that it offered her more hope than the last few days' worth of cryptic comments and lukewarm companionship.

"That was Kay on the phone this afternoon," she said at last, determined to draw him into conversation. Every one else had gone on to bed, and she knew that Trevor couldn't cover for her much longer before she'd have to get back to the cabin. "She had a dream that I was lost in darkness. That I had lost someone. She was afraid it was Joey."

He nodded, still not quite facing her, then sat down on the log nearest the fire. "What did you tell her?"

"I told her I hadn't lost Joey but I had managed to find him here. I told her to tell Dad we'd really chew things over when I got home."

He almost smiled. "I'm glad, Amy. Having you . . . get part of what you came here for almost makes it . . . worth it."

She didn't answer at first. She didn't want to force him to confess his turbulent feelings, but he owed her that much. He owed her more than his confession of grief; he owed her the whole truth.

And he gave it to her. "It's really very simple, Amy. The day you arrived, I realized instantly that my attraction to you was not . . . entirely . . . spiritual. I felt that the Lord had sent you here for a purpose, and I hoped that purpose was to give me joy. To ease my burdens." He chose his words with care. "To be my helpmate."

Amy could hardly breathe, let alone answer. It was just as well; Adam never gave her a chance.

"But almost immediately I discovered that you were crying out for ministry, and I was the only minister in sight. From the instant I heard you singing in the chapel, it was obvious to me—painfully, irrevocably obvious—that my duty to God and to you

159

lay in a single-file path that left no room for starlit walks holding hands.'' At last he faced her directly. "I accepted that reality the very day you came. I spent half the night reading the first chapter of James over and over again.'' His face was drawn and tight. "I've devoted myself to returning you to Jesus this week, Amy. And I refuse to let anyone—including you—prevent me from accomplishing that mission.''

Amy swallowed and studied the logs that still were hissing in the fire. "I don't suppose it occurred to you to ask me how I felt about . . . all of this.''

He rose abruptly. "I don't mean to belittle your feelings, Amy, but when it comes down to a choice between your wishes and the Lord's, you come in second place. Can you try to understand that?''

"Yes, I can. What I don't understand is what makes you so sure that God and I aren't on the same side on this one. If He sent me here—to you—isn't it possible that He wanted us to be close enough for you to . . . influence me as much as possible? Don't you think I'd focus more on Him and less on you if I weren't . . . so . . . torn up from the way you've been treating me?''

She had never meant to word it like that, never meant to give so much of herself away. But she suspected that he knew all along that she loved him. He seemed to know everything else about her.

He was standing with his back to her now, his eyes on the rise at the top of the bowl. She had to turn on her log to watch him; he was only a few feet away.

"Amy, I already apologized for acting like a jealous fool. I've encouraged you and Trevor to be together because I thought you might be able to uplift each other and because I . . . I thought I could endure this week a little better if you weren't . . . so clearly waiting for me.''

She gasped. Was it really so obvious?

"But it's untenable watching you with him,'' he

160

whispered, his voice so full of pain she could hardly bear to listen.

"I'm only trying to carry out your wishes, Adam! You asked me to help him! You know he's not the man I want!" Her voice rose in frustration. "I don't know where it could lead, Adam, but if you'd just give me a chance . . . give us a chance—"

"No! I told you before—"

"This isn't a summer fling I'll forget in September when I put away my swimsuit and take out my winter coats! I love you, Adam! Doesn't that mean anything to you?" The words were out before she could call them back.

They hit the man before her like a swinging ax, and he sank down before her on the nearest log. His elbows flanked his knees, and his head dropped hopelessly between his hands. Grief lined every muscle in his body.

"Your love means a great deal to me, Amy," he whispered, his voice husky and low. "But it just isn't worth the price."

"How can you be so sure? You've never even given me a chance! You—"

"I gave Linda a chance. I gave her three dozen chances and she wasn't even at war with the Lord!" His head snapped up to face her. "She couldn't face life as a minister's wife and neither can you."

This time it was Amy who was paralyzed. Not even a wisp of a retort found its way to her mind.

"It's all very simple, Amy," he started again, his voice laced with pain. "I fell madly in love with Linda near the end of my junior year in college. She started going to church with me, and I have to admit I never particularly questioned her religious background. She just *seemed* to believe what I believed, at the time that was good enough. She went home for the summer not too long after we got together. I—" he paused with some embarrassment, "I asked her to marry me before she left."

161

Amy knew she didn't want to hear the rest of this story. It could only get worse. But the sound of Adam's voice, so tortured, so full of the need for Grace, kept her at her post.

"Up till then I'd planned to teach history . . . in high school. I loved kids and books and trying to sort out people who just needed a friendly ear. I was also very active in the church youth group and helped out as liturgist when they needed me, so when the minister went on vacation in August he asked me if I'd like to preach one Sunday. I was a bit stunned at first, but he assured me that a university church had a right to expect an occasional sermon from a young person, and he really felt I had a lot to say." He smiled almost grimly. "I think poor old Dr. Phil spent more time helping me with that sermon than he spent on his vacation, but I did my very best. I did all right— nothing stupendous, no instant conversions—but it was a respectable first attempt. And somewhere in the middle of it, as clear as I'm sitting her talking to you, the Lord began to applaud me and said, 'This is it for you, Adam Reed. This is your path.' "

Again he grimaced, tugging at his hair. "Of course I thought I was just a bit dingy with the excitement of surviving my first sermon, but the feeling wouldn't seem to go away. When Dr. Phil got back we talked about it, and he just smiled a lot as though he'd known perfectly well I was supposed to be a minister all along. My folks felt the same way. By the time school started in September I was already checking out seminaries, but I waited to tell Linda in person because it just seemed to special a decision to write in a letter."

He shook his head. Amy tried to imagine him at twenty-one, innocent, eager to serve the Lord. She felt a brush of tears, and this time she knew they weren't for herself.

"Well, Linda was stunned, to say the least. But our

reunion was so delirious that it took me a while to figure that out. In fact, it took me several weeks to realize that Linda was doing her best to talk me out of the ministry. Finally, in November, she told me flatly that as much as she loved me, she could not, *would* not, marry a minister. Period."

Amy stifled a gasp. Adam glanced at her, just once, before he set his sights on a towering redwood to the north. The look on his face was terrible.

"Much to my discredit, I spent the next few months trying to convince myself that I really didn't want to be a pastor. We began to plan a June wedding." He shook his head. How well Amy could understand his youthful quandary! Slowly he looked at Amy, his gaze steady but slow. "You see, Amy, I wasn't just speaking idle words when I promised you that God forgives *everything*."

Amy nodded just once before he mercifully looked away. He took a few steps away from her and picked up a tiny rock to fiddle with as he talked. He did not continue right away.

"She left me right after Christmas. Because she really *did* love me, Amy, enough to know she was helping me make a terrible mistake. It takes a very special kind of woman to be a minister's wife, and it takes a very special kind to admit that she doesn't have that much courage." He paused to let his point sink in. "Dr. Phil helped me work through my pain over losing Linda, and more importantly, my guilt over turning my back on the Lord. Not . . . not to the extent you did, Amy. . . . I didn't stop believing in Him; I never missed a week in church; I didn't break any commandments. But I broke covenant with the Lord by turning my back on the task he'd set before me. And I will never . . . ," his haunted eyes engraved this message on Amy's heart, ". . . *never* do that again."

After that the silence was eerie. Amy wanted to run

163

away yet again, but his demand for her understanding bound her to the log until he released her. She wanted a broom to sweep up the shattered bits of faith and hope strewn over the bowl—Adam's as well as her own—but she could do nothing. She ached to pray for him, but even that simple task was beyond her.

Adam moved a little closer and leaned against a tall pine. "Have you ever given much thought to the demands of being a pastor's wife, Amy? Linda did. She didn't want to spend every Thanksgiving with some lonesome stranger at the family table. She didn't want to pray at the ladies' luncheons and take over the preaching when I had laryngitis. She didn't want to have every picnic and party interrupted with some last minute emergency—somebody dying, somebody hurting . . . some squeaky church wheel needing some pastorly grease. She was afraid I'd feel called to some Godforsaken continent without running water to heal the lame and give hope to the hopeless. She could not understand that the call of the Lord comes first with me—will always come first with me—and I cannot, *will not*, ever walk hand in hand with a woman who cannot *walk hand in hand with the Lord*."

For several moments Amy said nothing. She'd begged him for the truth, and now that he'd told her, she wished she'd stayed in darkness. A set of crickets began to chirp as Adam snapped twigs in his nervous hands.

"I do understand, Adam," she breathed into the night air. "No woman who loved you would ever try to steer you from your path." She swallowed hard and tried to go on. "But just because Linda wasn't strong enough to walk beside you doesn't mean that I won't be. She was terribly young and—"

"You're not listening, Amy! We're talking about the rest of your life on earth and your spirit for all eternity! We're talking about my promise to God to return you safely to Him whether you want to be returned or not! Compared to that nothing that happens between us—nothing that could ever happen between us—means anything at all!''

For a minute Amy said nothing. She was losing him; she had lost him. It was already too late, but still she had to try. ''But I do want to return to Him, Adam. I've made more than one step down that trail. You know that. Isn't it possible that . . . once I've found my way home . . . we could . . . approach each other somewhat differently?'' When he didn't answer, she pressed on. ''Can't you even give me that?''

''No.'' His voice held no quarter.

''Why? You said you wanted me. You said—''

''I said I would deliver you to the Lord! You're not going to find Him while you're waiting for me. He's not a means to an end—a quick conversion to make you acceptable as the local minister's lady. There is only one reason you should be seeking the Lord and only one motive pure enough to be worthy of you, Amy.''

She lowered her eyes in the face of his anger.

''When the Light fills your heart, you won't have to give me pretty speeches. You'll be somebody so different it will be as though this conversation never took place. So don't wait for miracles. I'm not your problem—and I'm not your solution. I'm just a servant trying to do my best, and I can only serve one Master.'' He stopped and glared at her. ''Now do you understand?''

She stood up and tossed back her head in newfound anger. She understood. She had underestimated his faith and overestimated his compassion; but at last she understood. ''I understand that you don't think I'm good enough for you, Adam Reed. And frankly, now that I've got that, I don't think either of us have to worry about this problem anymore. I'm fresh out of hunger for a man who's so eager to look down his nose at me from his lofty perch on the top of the cross. I suggest you take some time to read the Bible's view on humility. In your eagerness to please the Lord you seem to have forgotten some of His most basic rules!''

He could have denied her accusation. He could have told her that he didn't really think she wasn't good enough for him; he could have repeated his noble speech of loyalty to the Lord. He could have broken down and told her he wanted her anyway, and God and His orders would simply have to go on hold.

Instead he looked right through her, as he might have studied a Christmas present before it was unwrapped. Then he put her on the highest, dustiest shelf of his mind and closed the closet door.

She was sure she heard the clink of the key in the fire as he started up the rise.

CHAPTER 11

FOR AT LEAST TWO HOURS Amy thrashed about in her bunk, trying to stifle the noise of her tears. At last she gave up, crawling from her sleeping bag in silence as she groped about for Adam's Bible. She would find the passage on humility! She would show him. . . .

Of course she did no such thing. She snuck out to the front porch where the tiniest of wall lanterns illuminated the Holy Book, yet still she could not read it. Instead she buried her face against the leather and sobbed for fifteen minutes without restraint.

In hindsight she knew she'd done everything wrong. Adam had offered her his honesty, not his love; he had upheld his integrity, not his personal needs. She, in return, had responded selfishly, embarrassing them both with her childlike display. After hours and hours of rehashing his words, she knew why Adam had not refuted her final accusation. Not for a moment did she truly believe he thought he was too good for her, or superior to any other person. He simply knew that prolonging the scene between them would avail him nothing, and shatter what was left of his inner peace. He was a strong man, but his resolve was weakening. She knew that if there was any way at all he could justify his love for her, he would do it.

But he could not. And underneath the pain and the hurt and the impotent self-reproach, she had to admire his courage. The simple truth was that he loved her *too much* to sacrifice her heavenly future for his earthly pleasure. He knew that even if he could set aside the realities of her spiritual needs, sooner or later their future would catch up to them. Without a massive change in Amy's heart, he risked a rerun of his loss of Linda.

The hardest part for Amy was facing the truth he'd declared about her return to the Lord. Adam could help her do it, but he could not be the reason she sought such redemption. It was a strong motive but an erroneous one, and she knew that she must give up the futile dream of a life with him, once and for all, if she was ever to be whole again.

After a while the evening breeze caressed her and began to dry her tears. The leather cover seemed to warm her fingers. The Bible waited in her hands.

She didn't really let herself decide. She just opened the Book, brushing the red-rimmed pages, feeling the majesty of the secrets within. No longer did she want to teach Adam a lesson, or to prove to herself that she still remembered where certain passages could be found. Now she read in search of a kind of comfort that only those delicate parchment pages could offer her . . . the only place on earth where such comfort could be found.

She started with Isaiah, longing to see in print Adam's promise that God had not forgotten her. The words were there, just as she remembered them. Only sweeter. And the words that followed were like food to her troubled body . . . pages and pages of Isaiah and then the book of Amos, the prophet who, like Amy, had failed to hear the Lord's voice for so long.

She read the Psalms, each and every one of them, and then the four Gospels, which had waited for her without changing for seven endless years.

"How did I live without this?" she whispered to the night as the lacy pages rustled in her hands. "How did I greet each day without praising Him with 'harp and lyre'? How did I go to sleep each night without the words of John?"

She read the story of Creation, when God gave Adam's rib to Eve. She studied Joshua to learn how the Israelites crossed the Jordan River to reach God's chosen land of milk and honey, just as she herself would have to cross a Jordan of her own to reach His kingdom. She even braved the book of James to feel the strength of Adam's fight against temptation. By the trickle of light from the porch lantern she fed on the Word for hour after hour, reading and discovering while the anguish peeled off her soul in layers of Grace. She was totally unprepared for the voice that spoke behind her.

"Would you maybe like some company?"

"Tiffany!" Amy was stunned. "What on earth are you doing up? It's three o'clock in the morning!"

"I know. But you've been gone so long I was beginning to wonder if I should go get Daddy. I didn't know you were right out front."

Amy was alarmed. "Is something wrong with one of the girls? Is somebody sick? Is—"

"No." Tiffany shook her head. "But you came back from the bowl looking like you were about to die, and you haven't gone to sleep at all. When you just disappeared I thought you might have . . . well, run away."

It was the longest speech Tiffany had ever made to Amy, and though she knew the girl hadn't worded her fears with precise accuracy, her perception of another person's pain was remarkable.

"I think I'm done running away, Tiffany."

"You mean 'cause you're a grownup?"

"No, not exactly. There's more than one way to run away from a problem. Grownups just have more ways to go about it."

She didn't know whether or not Tiffany understood, but the girl shut the door behind her and sat down on the steps next to Amy. "I know. My daddy ran away." Her eyes were dark. "Did he tell you about it?"

Amy struggled for honesty. "He told he he was ashamed of how he handled things after your mother died. He's terribly sorry he left you alone for so long."

"I wasn't alone," Tiffany countered. "I was lucky I had Grandma after he dumped me."

"Tiffy!" Amy was appalled. "You don't really think he just . . . forgot you altogether, do you?"

For a long time Tiffany was silent. "He just ran off and left me, Amos. Mama was dead and he just went away. How did he expect me to feel?"

Without thinking, Amy slipped her arm around the little girl. "Someday, Tiffy, you need to tell him how you feel about that. In the meantime maybe we just need to thank God that he finally found the courage to come back."

The child wriggled out of the maternal embrace and abruptly changed the subject. "Sometimes I wish I could run away from Julie Ann. Why do you think she follows me around all the time?"

Amy smiled. "She probably likes you."

Tiffany shook her head. "You said nobody liked me. You said I was a baby."

With great caution, Amy took the little girl's hand. "I wanted you to have a good time here, Tiffany. I wanted you to be happy. Maybe I didn't go about it the right way, but you were making it awfully hard for me."

She was surprised when the tiny fingers squeezed

170

her hand. "I know. I'm not very nice sometimes. I don't really know why." She lifted her face to Amy's. "I don't want to be awful."

Overruling her common sense, Amy gave her a quick hug. "If you were awful Julie Ann wouldn't be so eager to be your friend, and I wouldn't worry about you so much."

"You worry about me?"

"I do. And I worry about you dad."

Afraid she'd said the wrong thing, Amy was still. But Tiffany's next response surprised her. "Sometimes I worry about him, too. I don't think he knows what he wants."

Amy had to agree. "But I'm sure he wants to be with you, Tiff. He just isn't quite sure how to show it."

Tiffany didn't answer, but after a moment she yawned and stood up. "I'm awful sleepy, Amos. Can we go to bed now?"

Instantly Amy rose, a new idea forming in her mind. "Of course. We've got a long hike in the morning, and it's important that we feel just super."

Tiffany grinned. Amy followed her into the cabin, carefully laying Adam's Bible at the foot of her bed. Then she trailed the little girl to her own bunk and tucked her in for the night. She zipped up the sleeping bag and gave her tiny blond termagant a kiss on the cheek.

Without a word of protest, Tiffany put both arms around Amy's neck and hugged her goodnight.

It was almost nine o'clock in the morning when they finally got on the trail. While Amy had expected most of the last minute snafus that had held them up, she had depleted every last nuance of patience during morning watch—playing the perfect choir leader with Adam—and she was noticeably edgy by the time they started counting noses in the meadow.

171

It didn't help any that she was working on less than three hours of sleep. The great sense of Scriptural euphoria that had filled her in the wee small hours of the night did not seem to be sustaining itself this morning, but she suspected that part of that was because Adam, hovering about like a mother hen, had insisted on devoting his morning to seeing them off.

"We won't forget to brush our teeth, Dad, and we'll be sure to write," Trevor finally told him after he'd checked each lunch, each sweat shirt, and each pint-sized pair of sensible shoes. "Relax, Adam! We'll be back in time for a dip in the pool before dinner."

"I hope everybody has a great time."

And then, quite suddenly, he was standing by Amy's side. "Do you have everything you need?"

"Yes." She did not look at him.

His voice was low and troubled as he asked, "Are you . . . are you up to this, Amy?"

"What does that mean?" she snapped, growing irritated by his concern. "I told you I've hiked this trail a dozen times—"

"But never when you were in such a reckless mood."

She faced him squarely. "Are you or aren't you the same man who told me just three days ago that he wouldn't lose a wink of sleep if his daughter was in my cabin?"

"I am." His eyes never left her face. "You know I trust you, Amy. I'm just asking you to . . . be careful." He tried to laugh. "I'm going to be a terrible father. I'll worry every minute my kids are out of my sight."

They could have been our children, Adam, her eyes reproached him. *Now their mother will be some holy woman I've never met . . . someone whose faith is as stalwart as yours. . . .*

She was certain that Adam could read her thoughts, but he said nothing. Yet while they stood together, his

172

face grew dark in syncopation with the sudden gust of wind that swept across the meadow as the sky turned gray. Moments passed while Amy waited to be dismissed, but still he watched her. Pain took the place of the joy she'd always loved to witness in his ethereal blue eyes. No words passed between them before he turned away.

"See you all at supper," he called out to the kids as he strolled across the meadow.

"Goodbye, Summit!" the tiny hikers called out in unison. "We'll bring you back a pine cone from the top!"

Amy took a deep breath and marched quickly toward the trail.

Trevor followed with less haste and more caution.

"Well, we're on our way. At last," he announced with a smile, placing his feet on the crooked trail with care as they left the comforting circle of the lodge. "I'm really looking forward to this, Amy."

She scavenged a smile from some hidden closet of her heart but could not manage to reply.

"How long do you think it will take us to get to the top?"

Amy shrugged. She wasn't worried about getting *up* the mountain. It was after they got back down that she'd have to face Adam again, praising the Lord while she sat beside him at the bowl. It would not be easy to encourage all these lovely children to celebrate this camp and mourn their last night's nostalgia when all she wanted to do was cut and run for home! Worse yet, Holy Communion was scheduled for this last night, and she was obligated to lead her tiny choir in a heartwarming rendition of "Let Us Break Bread Together on Our Knees." It wasn't going to be easy.

"Traditionally the trip up took until lunch and we still got home in time for a swim before dinner," she told Trevor. "But Adam says that the trail hasn't been checked this season and there's a rumor that it was

173

left in a pretty sad state after last winter's flooding. So . . . it's anybody's guess."

Trevor lost his footing for just a second, leaning on Amy, before he stood upright and asked, "You don't think we'll have any trouble getting up there, ~~do~~ you?"

"Of course not. I could hike this trail in my sleep." Again her tone was sharper than she would have liked, and her confidence was less than her haughty words implied. She did remember the trail, of course, but it had been seven years . . . seven years of rain, boisterous young trailblazers, inconsistent maintenance and . . . ? "I'm going up to the front, Trevor, just to make sure nobody gets too far ahead. You bring up the rear and make sure we don't lose anybody."

"Yes ma'am."

She tossed him a quick glance to make sure the playful note of respect didn't hide a twinge of resentment. But his expression indicated relief that Amy was still in charge of the expedition and willing to condone his featherbedding.

Amy brushed past the children rather briskly, eager to set a pace that would give her some space from the others. She needed the time to reconnoiter the trail; she needed the time alone.

She didn't get it. Tiffany instantly attached herself to Amy's heels like a horseshoe magnet and was not about to let her escape. It was the young girl who pointed out the first fork in the trail.

"Look, Amos," she announced about thirty minutes after they left the main camp. "There's a split in the road up there. It looks like it goes straight up the mountain, but it's almost too steep and skinny to be a trail."

Amy had to agree with her. For several moments she stared at the tiny path, trying to remember where it led. "I think it's a shortcut through all these hairpin curves. Either way we still head toward the top."

174

Tiffany nodded as though she'd covered the same ground many times before. "You're not going to take it, are you? Even if the little kids could make it, I don't think my dad could."

Amy swung back to face her in surprise. Under the layers of hostile self-protection this child hid a lot of concern for others. Secretly Amy suspected that Tiffany's clinginess this morning stemmed from some private determination that Amy shouldn't be left to suffer alone.

After a minute Tiffany asked almost indifferently, "You want me to go check it out and get back to you?"

Oh, my sweet little tomboy Tiffany. There's nobody I'd rather have by me in a pinch, Amy whispered in her heart.

"That's okay, Tiff," she said out loud. "We're in not great hurry. We'll just take the long way."

And it was the long way. It got longer and longer as the day went on. Joey managed to get a blister and spent half an hour soliciting sympathy for his reddened heel. Julie Ann tripped and slid maybe three feet off the trail, skinning her knees and elbows enough to justify some quick tears. She refused to take another step until Tiffany looked her over and declared her fit for travel. At one point a child reported that the Giraffe had broken his ankle. While Amy had no doubts that this was a gross exaggeration, she was surprised to learn that Trevor had slipped on a steep curve almost half an hour before she got the news. Because he was so near the end of the snakelike line of hikers, nobody had even noticed his problem until he got back up.

"Rest stop," Amy called, even though Trevor assured her that he was fine. "I wanted to wait till we reached the clearing by the North Fork, but I think we better take a breather now."

Everyone nodded in agreement and slumped down

175

on the ground. Amy really wasn't sure what the problem was. They all seemed tired except for her! And she was working on the skimpiest night's sleep. She discounted the possibility that the grinding agony of Adam's challenging words was what was goading her to set such an intense pace. They'd planned this hike in spite of him. By golly, they'd enjoy every minute of it!

It was already noon by the time they reached the North Fork clearing. Amy had expected it to be oppressively hot by now, but the day had turned cloudy and more than a little gray. There was no sign at the clearing to indicate which of the three new roads led to the summit. Again Amy stopped the group to rest.

"How much longer is it, Amy?" Trevor asked with genuine exhaustion. "I don't think I bargained for this when I agreed to this little sojourn."

"Really, Trevor, you'd think you were crippled and a hundred and three." She knew she wasn't being very supportive, but her inner torment made it hard to be tolerant of another's suffering. "We always had a solid break at the clearing, and then reached the summit, in less than an hour."

"Another hour?" he groaned. "I'm already wilted."

"Hush," she told him unsympathetically. "It'll be a lot easier going back down the hill."

As soon as Trevor hobbled off to his rock, Amy scrambled over to the intersection of trails and tried to sort them out. One clearly led off to the west and down the side of the mountain. But the other two both led up the hill, and no portion of Amy's memory prompted her as to the direction of the summit.

"You're lost, aren't you?" Tiffany questioned, handing Amy a broken piece of redwood that had once been part of the trail sign. "We're going in circles."

"We are *not* going in circles. We are going up the mountain. The summit is this way."

With confidence born of desperation, Amy struck out on the path to the left, and in time her raggle-taggle band slowly followed her. Joey was limping along beside Trevor, nursing his tiny blister with great ado, and several of the other children had started to complain as well.

"Amy!" Joey cried out plaintively. "Can you come back here and walk with me?"

"No," she called back a bit too shortly. "I've got to lead the group. You'll be fine. Don't act like a baby over a tiny blister."

She regretted the words as soon as she called them out, but she was too far away to offer Joey a private apology. She was nervous and tired and generally irritated already, and the exhausted children and uncertain turns weren't helping any.

It occurred to Amy rather dismally that this entire journey was beginning to resemble her upward trek in search of God. Rocks and brambles kept getting in the way; others on the same trail were falling. Darkness seemed to shroud her path, but the promise of light lingered at some distant spot, high above her on the trail.

Amy knew only one cure for darkness. Almost without conscious thought, she began to sing.

Old Noah built himself an ark;
There's one more river to cross.
He built it out of hickory bark;
There's one more river to cross.

One more river!
And that's the river of Jordan!
One more river!
There's one more river to cross!

By now the children were accustomed to singing with Amy, and they lifted up her spirits with their voices almost instantly. Tiffany, still right behind her, sang more loudly than the others to help set the tone. Within minutes the entire mood of the group was transformed. Even Amy began to shake some of the gloom that had trailed her since her last encounter with Adam. She was certain that they were nearing the top of the mountain. Even though she couldn't see any indication that they were close to a summit, she remembered that Persistence Peak came upon hikers rather suddenly just about an hour after they left the clearing. Her watch gave hope to the momentary end of the journey.

She had just launched the group into an enthusiastic rendition of "We Are Climbing Jacob's Ladder," when the trail abruptly turned left . . . down, inexorably down, down, the hill. Even from this height Amy could see its eventual destination . . . a magnificent tumbling waterfall that would be impossible for anyone over the age of three to forget.

She had never seen it before.

CHAPTER 12

BY THE TIME THEY RETURNED to the North Fork clearing, it was after one o'clock. Without consulting Amy, Trevor told the kids, "This is as far as we go, guys. Sit down, eat lunch, and go to sleep. You've had enough."

Amy knew he was right. She should have let them eat the first time they'd reached the clearing. She should have doubled-checked with someone to refresh her memory on the unmarked trail! She should have paced them slower right from the start.

"I'm sorry, Trevor," she managed to force out when they were alone. "This is all my fault."

Trevor managed a wan smile. "No harm done, Amy, but I don't think anybody but you is determined to reach the summit. We just needed a destination. We've had a long hike now, and we still ought to be able to get back before supper . . . assuming my legs don't go into hibernation if I sit down for a while."

Amy drew back in some surprise. "You mean you're giving up on the summit? We can't be more than an hour away and there's only one trail left!

Besides, there's a main road back down from Persistence Peak that's much easier than this trail. We'd get there just as early—"

"No." It was the first time he'd ever refused to follow her lead. "Be reasonable, Amy. The kids are exhausted. Joey's been limping on that blister for an hour, and Julie Ann still sheds a few tears every now and again because her knees are really hurting. I don't even think you noticed that once I had to wait almost five minutes for Roger to catch his breath before we could catch up with the rest of you. He's too proud to complain, but he's shot." He glared at Amy for emphasis. "They're all shot. And I'm dead on my feet. The only reason you could possibly want to go one now is to save your pride with Adam."

He was right, of course, but that in itself made her angry. She wasn't being fair to the kids, or to Trevor. But she didn't want to face Amy with the news that she couldn't even find her way up the mountain, let alone up the *Mountain*. She didn't want to face him at all.

It was Amy who looked away first, fighting a hot stinging mist in her eyes. Knowing Trevor could read far too much into her introspective silence, she snatched up her lunch sack in self-defense and marched over to an isolated rock on the far side of the clearing.

Lunch consisted of a bologna sandwich, an apple and a bag of potato chips. Wistfully she remembered the huge homemade chocolate chip cookies that were Irene the Queen's trademark. So many things had changed!

Halfway through her sandwich, it occurred to Amy that she hadn't said grace before the meal. Neither had the children. A week ago this would not have troubled her, but after a night spent with the Bible, it just seemed like one more inexcusable shortcoming.

I'd have to make them sing anyway, she told

herself. *I still don't think I can pray . . . especially before a group like this.*

Yet she suspected that if things had turned out differently with Adam, she would be praying by now. Every day she'd been at camp she'd recaptured some tiny part of her spiritual past, and that last piece of the puzzle had been about to fall into place . . . until her last talk with Adam.

We're talking about the rest of your life on earth and your spirit for all eternity. . . . Compared to that nothing that happens between us . . . means anything at all.

Adam's words—a lifetime of them crammed into this dizzying week—swirled around her mind as she tried to sort out his pastoral wisdom from his mortal man's anguish. But somehow she couldn't separate the two any more. In spite of everything, he was just Adam, the man she desperately loved. She didn't love him because he was a minister, or in spite of the fact. She didn't love him because he had the power to pave an easier road for her return to the Lord; she realized now that no one could walk that trail but Amy. But that road—or any other—would always be filled with more sunshine if she knew that Adam walked beside her . . . or waited at the other end.

But this afternoon he wouldn't be waiting for Amy Shelby. He'd be waiting for this week's counselor at Timber Wolf Cabin, who'd gotten off to a rocky start as a spiritual leader and ended up as a washout in the hiking department. It was hardly shaping up as a day she'd want to cherish and remember.

Amy's thoughts were still pretty grim when Tiffany plopped down beside her, uninvited.

"You messed up, huh?" was the child's greeting.

Amy swallowed several uncharitable retorts and simply nodded.

"I bet you feel pretty dumb."

This time Amy narrowed her eyes at the girl. "This

181

isn't my finest hour, Tiffany, and I most assuredly do not need you to rub it in."

Surprise reddened the youngster's face. "I didn't . . . I didn't mean to make you feel worse. I just . . . I thought maybe you shouldn't be alone right now. I mean, sometimes we all do stupid things we wish we could do over."

She nibbled on her lower lip, trying to gauge Amy's response to her tentative offer of comfort. She looked so sincere—and so *awkward*—that Amy just couldn't be mean. The girl had already proved her kind intentions more than once in the last two days.

"Thanks, Tiffy. I guess it isn't that big a deal. I'll get over it."

Tiffany nodded uncertainly. "I think the worst part about doing something stupid is . . . having to sit all by yourself and think about it all the time. It just gets worse and worse." She twisted a lock of her fine blond hair while hazy memories of pain darkened her blue eyes.

Amy chose her words with care. "You're right, Tiffany. When I first came to Camp Colina I was still hurting a lot over a mistake I made an awfully long time ago. Adam got me to talk about it and now I feel a lot better." She paused, trying to forget the last time she'd talked to Adam—when the sharing hadn't done her the slightest bit of good—then asked gently in the young girl's jargon, "What's the stupidest thing you ever did, Tiffy?"

She wanted to call her "honey," but she didn't dare scare the girl off with an endearment. As it was she was taking a chance. After all, it was daylight now and there were other people nearby. Amy could almost imagine Tiffany's haughty shrug as she declared that she never did silly things; she wasn't a baby. Instead, her eyes clouded for a minute as she picked up a pine needle and broke it in her hands. Then she looked right at Amy and whispered, "I told my dad it was his fault that my mother died."

Fresh anguish washed over Amy, but she forced herself to say nothing.

"She got sick in the middle of the night. He wasn't home yet—I don't know where he was. Neither did she. I tried to help her, but I was too little. I remember trying to open the front door to go get the lady next door, or something, but it was locked way up high. I didn't know how to use a phone. I couldn't do *nothing!*" This time her eyes welled with tears. "When he got home I was in bed with her, holding her close, but she was already dead. I remember her body feeling cold beside me. The minute I saw him I started to scream, and I kept screaming at him while he called the ambulance, the police, my grandmother. I know they gave me something to make me stop, but by then it was too late."

She sighed deeply. "Somebody brought me some clothes and toys from the house, but I never got to go home again. My dad just disappeared. When he showed last month I . . . I didn't know what to do." She was really crying now. "I hate him, Amos. But I love him. He's my dad! But he should have been there. He shouldn't have left her all alone."

This time Amy put her arms around the little girl, grateful for the privacy this little cove provided. The tiny body shook, each little rib as thin and fine as the pine needles in Tiffany's hands. Amy stroked the delicate blond hair and shed a few tears of her own. For several moments they were both silent before Amy whispered over the young head, "Have you ever told him any of this, honey? Have you ever tried to forgive him or let him know all the feelings fighting with each other inside of you?"

Tiffany shook her head, pressing harder into Amy's chest. "I tried to tell my grandma once. She said he was a terrible man! She said if he'd been home like he should have been, Mom wouldn't have died. And then I said that I was there, and I should have saved her, so maybe it was my fault and not his. But she said I was too little to do anything. I know that in my head, Amos . . . ," she lifted a tearful face to Amy and rubbed knuckles into her reddened eyes, " . . . but I still think I should have done something. Sometimes I think it's my fault, not his, and then I hate him for making me feel that way." She started to tremble. "I don't know what to do, Amos. I want to hate him but he's my *daddy*." Two huge tears stumbled down her cheeks before she whispered, "I don't want to lose him all over again."

For a long time Amy rocked her, sensing the darkness that seemed to close around them. When tiny raindrops brushed her face, Amy ignored them. They seemed to blend with her tears.

"Sweetheart, I can't get inside you and tell you what to feel. But I am so certain that things will never be all right between you and your dad until you sit down and talk and cry and hug each other. Forgive each other. Start over. Start fresh. I know how much he loves you! He's so ashamed of what he did, honey. He's just desperate for you to give him another chance."

"I know that," Tiffany declared with wisdom beyond her years. "Sometimes I want to make it easy on him. Then sometimes I want to hurt him for what he did. To her . . . and to me."

"But look who's doing the hurting, Tiffany? Look what you're doing to yourself!"

Tiffany sniffed and began to pull away.

"Honey—listen to me. It was my fault that my mother died—I mean *really* my fault, and there's no way I can pretend otherwise. When my father got married again, I hated his new wife because she wasn't my mother. I even resented Joey."

"Joey?" Tiffany looked surprised. "He's not so bad."

Amy smiled. "I couldn't stand the sight of him!" she declared with feeling.

For a moment she stopped, certain that she heard footsteps approaching the tiny glen. But the only eavesdropper she could see was a squirrel chattering beneath a nearby pine.

Tiffany shook her head and declared with feeling. "Joey just thinks you're the greatest, Amos. Everybody here thinks he's your real brother."

The squirrel scampered off with a great splash of dry leaves. This time Amy didn't even bother to look at the tiny animal.

"He is now, sweetheart. When I began to forgive myself I began to forgive everybody else for whatever they did or didn't do. I'm starting over now—I'm trusting God to help me start over—and I can't believe how different I feel." The minute she said it, Amy knew it was true. She didn't have Adam, but she did have Jesus. She wasn't alone anymore.

Tiffany's lovely blue eyes sought Amy's for a moment. She sat up a little straighter. "I don't know about . . . God. My mother really believed in Him, but Daddy never did. I mean, not really. Sometimes he went to church with us on Christmas or Easter, but he just did it to make Mom happy. That's why it's so *weird* for him to be so . . . gung-ho about Camp Colina and all."

Amy stroked the girl's fine hair as her mother must once have done, feeling a deep kinship with the woman. "People do change, sweetheart. Don't you think it's possible that your dad has done some . . . pretty serious thinking about what really matters to him since your mother died? I don't think it's an accident that he came back to see you right now. I don't think it's an accident that he brought you here to camp. He really needs to make things right with you, Tiffy . . . and with God. I think you dad needs you every bit as much as you need him."

"He doesn't need me!" she shot back, her old defensiveness forming a quick new shell around her bared feelings. "And I don't need him, either! He's just—"

"Tiffany?" Trevor's voice cut across his daughter's, as if from a distance. "Is Amy there with you?"

She frowned at the interruption, then called out stiffly, "Yes."

A moment later Trevor shuffled into view, dragging his left foot as though he were in pain. He looked irritated with both of them, and Amy wondered how much he'd overheard. If Tiffany was thinking along similar lines, she didn't show it. Her opening words to her father were, "You're hurt."

He tossed her a pained glance, then turned to Amy without acknowledging his daughter's comment. "Look, Amy, I know you like to run your own show but you could at least bother to talk to me when I send a messenger. It's long past time to be going and —"

"What messenger? I didn't know you wanted to leave. And what's wrong with your foot? I know you said you were tired but—"

"I'm more than tired!" he exploded. "I'm sick of this whole stupid hike. I hurt my ankle when I slipped on the trail, and when I tried to get up a few minutes ago it just folded right under me. So I sent Joey to get you and since you never showed up, I had to come over here myself. Now the kids are restless and I'm ready for a stretcher, so let's get a move on, lady."

Silence held the three of them. Amy could not believe that Trevor did not recognize signs of grief on his daughter's face, yet he made no move to comfort her. Still, Tiffany was the next one to speak—in Amy's defense.

"It's not her fault, Dad. Joey never told her you wanted to see her."

"I saw him come over here! I watched him come right to this rock and stop as though he heard you talking and didn't want to interrupt! But that was five minutes ago—"

He turned wondering eyes on the look that passed between Amy and his daughter. Together they whispered, "*The squirrel!*"

"Excuse me—"

"Go find him, Tiffy," Amy ordered tersely, ignoring Trevor's confusion. "I've got to make him understand."

Instantly Tiffany scampered off, fully understanding Amy's urgency. Trevor did not.

"Would you mind explaining the mystical hold you seem to be gaining over my daughter?" he demanded peevishly, forgetting how grateful he'd been for that blossoming relationship just yesterday when he'd heard about Tiffany's performance in Amy's Bible class. "I brought her up here to establish a new relationship with *me*, not a camp counselor she'll never see again. If there's anything she's told you that would help—"

"Nothing I could tell you could begin to mitigate the damage I would do if I broke her confidence, Trevor. I know you're doing your best. So is she. Give her time."

He mumbled an angry retort just before Tiffany rejoined them. She looked breathless and more than a little frightened.

"He's not here, Amos."

Serpentine panic laced itself around Amy's throat. "What do you mean he's not here?"

"I looked all over the clearing. I called out on each trail. Nobody's seen him since he talked to Dad." She stared at Amy, new tears glistening. "He heard us. I know it. He didn't understand."

"I'm the one who doesn't understand," Trevor cut in. "What did who hear? You mean Joey? What—"

Again Amy ignored him, kneeling down in front of Tiffany. "It's not your fault, honey. I should have thought before I talked up here—"

"You just said it to make me feel better! If I hadn't

started talking you never would have said it and Joey'd still be here!"

"Tiffany—we'll find him."

"No we won't!" she burst out in sudden panic. "He ran away and we'll never find him and it's all my fault!"

Her words echoed Amy's feelings so precisely that she could hardly refute the young girl. But she forced herself to be strong. "You stay with your dad. I'll find Joey."

With that she marched off, leaving the bewildered Trevor to cope with his high-strung daughter. By now Amy was consumed only with thoughts of Joey; she was surprised to find the clearing full of youngsters hopping about in eagerness to go home.

"Are we going home now, Amos? I'm tired. Do you think we'll have time to swim before dinner?"

She scanned them all, each tiny face, and read the fatigue painted there for anyone to see. She should have taken them home hours ago! She shouldn't have taken them on this hike at all. It was her own search for the summit of her life, her struggle to return to that magical pinnacle of peace she'd once found at Camp Colina. She had never intended to offer Joey as a sacrificial lamb.

"Time to count noses," she declared with artificial cheer, calling out in loud tones designed for Joey's benefit. "As soon as everybody's lined up we'll start back." Instantly dust choked the clearing as the children scuttled into rows before her. She tried to honor each tiny face, read the trust and weariness there, but all she really sought was that one sunny face with curly brown hair . . . the one little face that was missing.

"Joeeeeeeey!" she called out after they were all assembled. "We're going home!"

A thunderclap answered, causing Amy to shiver. She'd almost forgotten the quiet raindrops that had

188

mixed with her tears. "Come on, sweetheart!" she tried again. "It's late and everybody's tired! I'll carry you if your foot still hurts!"

The children stared at her, first in irritation and then, slowly, in concern.

"You mean Joey's really *gone*?" Julie Ann whined. "What are we going to do?"

Amy met Trevor's eyes across the pine-scented cove and read new alarm there. Ignoring him, she abandoned the rows of children and began to patrol the trails that led off the main clearing, calling for Joey up and down each spike.

Her words grew more desperate as each minute passed. Finally she was calling bluntly, "I love you, Joey! I was only telling Tiffany how it used to be a long time ago! Please let me explain!"

The redwoods listened sagely but offered no reply. A lazy afternoon sun cast tentative shadows across the clearing, hinting that darkness would take the mountains early this evening. The sky had a dark, angry look to it in spite of the lingering sunlight.

Trevor looked like a thundercloud himself. "We've got to take these kids home, Amy," he declared, pulling her out of earshot of the increasingly worried children. "Even if we don't get lost, it'll be dark by the time we get back to camp. We aren't going to find Joey this way. We need some kind of help. That's Adam's bailiwick. Let him turn out the hounds."

"But Trevor, I can't just leave him here! He's so little. He's so—"

"Look, Amy, I'm afraid for Joey, too. But I don't want to end up with nineteen other kids in the same predicament! We've got to get them to safety. There's nothing else to do!"

Amy closed her eyes and fought back tears of fear and self-reproach. Trevor was right; of course he was right. "All right. Take them home. Tell Adam what happened. I'll stay here and keep looking."

"Amy!" He was appalled. "You'll do no such thing."

"Why not?"

"In the first place, it's bad enough that we've lost Joey . . . I don't want to lose you too. In the second place," he looked embarrassed, "I don't know if I *can* get them home. You took a lot of unmarked turns and most of the time I was nursing my ankle. About the last thing I want to do is get lost on some hairpin curve in the dark with nineteen cold, hungry, footsore little kids!"

Amy wanted to scream her exasperation. She wanted to shout out her guilt and her fear. She would happily have thrown herself into the waterfall if Joey and the other children could just be delivered safely back to Adam.

And then a little voice, Tiffany's little voice, reacher her anguished ears. "I can get them back, Amos," she declared with quiet confidence. "I know every turn you made. I even helped you decide some of them."

Amy met those wide, blue eyes and realized that Tiffany, confused and uncertain as she was, honestly wanted to help someone other then herself and truly believed that she could. *Oh Jesus,* came Amy's unbidden prayer, *Let her do this thing. Let her help her father. Let her help the rest of us. Let her feel needed and worthwhile*.

"Oh, thank you, Tiffy!" she whispered, hugging the little girl. "You are an answer to prayer."

Just as the child began to swell with pride, her father said, "Are you crazy? She's just a—"

"Great guide and the only chance you have. She was with me every step of the way and has an eye like a hawk. Besides, most of the trail is straight down. You don't have any east-west decisions to make until you're nearly there."

"When it might already be dark."

Amy didn't answer at first, certain that anything else she said was sure to be wrong. She knew that Trevor was out of his depth, and she knew that his dilemma was entirely her fault. She wouldn't have blamed him for blowing up at her, but he managed to hold back the tide.

For several minutes he glared at Amy, then shifted his gaze to rest on his troubled but willing child. He struggled to give her a smile.

"Okay, Tiff," he relented. "You're in charge. I'm counting on you, honey."

Tiffany took a moment to inhale the pride in his voice, then scampered off the round up the children. Trevor studied Amy for another minute, then shook his head and took her in his arms. His brotherly hug healed the day's tension between them.

"I wish I could do more for you, Amy," he whispered. "One way or another I'll get these kids back to camp and then come back up here with Adam. We'll find Joey. I promise you. It's just a matter of time."

Amy hugged him back, trying not to cry. "I'm really not too sure I could get you down any better than Tiffany could," she confessed. "I've already made enough mistakes today. Just get going so you won't have nightfall to contend with. Tell Adam to start here and then head for the summit. If Joey's not hiding around here, that's probably where he'll be going. He may come out as soon as he really thinks we're leaving anyway. Maybe he just needed some time to cool down."

Amy wished she could have believed those brave words, but she could not. She stood perfectly still, trembling, after Tiffany started down the trail with a wave of tired and hungry young campers behind her, their voices already raised by the young girl's determined attempt at song. Reluctantly Trevor brought up the rear, limping heavily, his parched croak a valiant attempt to add to the music.

Amy listened until there was no human sound in the clearing; even the blue jays grew comatose in the cloudy silence. A brisk wind swept off the ever elusive mountains, and a new scattering of raindrops plummeted her from the sky. Early darkness, that single sure sign of a storm, begin to ink the emptiness around her until the shadows of the pines blended with the rocks and long-dead campfire near the cliff.

She had never felt so alone.

It was sheer folly to climb the cliff face toward the summit in the dark, but Amy didn't feel she had much choice. She had examined every bit of the trail near the clearing hours ago and was convinced that if Joey had been hiding there, he would surely have come out by now. Angry or not, he would be cold, scared and hungry. Amy certainly was!

There were still wisps of moonlight, so travel was not impossible as she scaled the mountain. This part of the trail did not appear to washed out, and she could not remember why she hadn't chosen this direction in the first place. Of course it was way to late for second guesses . . . too late to ponder Adam's reaction when he learned that she'd lost Joey. How heavily he'd felt the burden of safety for all his tiny charges! How diligently he'd warned her not to take this hike! How inexcusable that she'd managed to let him down!

But Amy was even more afraid of her father's reaction to the news . . . and Kay's anguish when she learned how closely her nightmare had foreshadowed tonight's reality. Surely Adam would have to let them know what had happened . . . assuming that Trevor managed to get the other children back with the message! Would they think she'd done it on purpose? Would either of them ever forgive her if something happened to Joey? Would she ever forgive herself?

Amy was glad she had a destination, even in the

dark, because otherwise she would have gone crazy. The coyotes were howling from a nearby peak, clearly preparing for their evening hunt. Other threatening snakelike sounds rustled from the bushes, and Amy's fearful imaginings did not allow her to consider them friendly omens.

Yet the trail to Persistence Peak—which had eluded her so cruelly all day—now seemed to be remarkably brief, and she was near the top of the mountain in less than half an hour. She reached it triumphantly, calling for Joey until she was hoarse. When her voice gave out, Amy stood perfectly still for nearly five minutes before she realized, with an abrupt exhalation of defeat, that she had achieved absolutely nothing.

It was then that she began to cry.

The tears came slowly at first, like the wheels of a train when the engine first begins to move. Then they strengthened in fear and fury as her body began to shake. She had bungled so many things, destroyed or damaged so many loving hopes by her inadequacies! She'd never given Kay a chance, never made a clean breast of things with her father! She'd grenaded her chance of lifelong happiness with Adam by her adolescent choice of misery outside of the Lord. And then there was little Joey . . . so full of sunshine and innocence! He'd done nothing to deserve the pain she'd inflicted upon him, let alone the pain he might now be feeling from the cold, the storm, the coyotes. . . .

"Help me!" she begged to no one, falling to her knees in the now-soggy earth. "I just can't fix this up alone. I just don't know what to do!"

A sudden comfort wrapped itself around her, and she realized wonderingly that it was the remembered warmth of Adam. Adam, who would unquestionably help her when Trevor told him the news. Adam, who was probably on his way here right now with all the help she could possibly need. Adam, who would tell her without equivocation to *get down on her knees and pray*.

She was already on her knees, but Amy knew that was the easy part. She was absolutely certain that the Lord had long since given up listening for the sound of her tortured voice. She covered her face with her hands, aching to pray but sure she could not. The mud seemed to suck her ever more deeply into the ground.

Then Adam's voice reached out almost palpably to touch her. It was so warm, so loving, so . . . full of the spirit. A dozen special moments filled the memory of her heart. Mornings touched by sunshine . . . nights warmed by fellowship and Christian song. Honesty even when it hurt . . . hellos and goodbyes graced with dimpled smiles and hugs. She could remember every nuance of faith in his eyes the first time he'd quoted Scripture to her: " 'I have engraved you on the palms of my hands.' "

Amy traced her thumbs over her palms, toying with the image. But it was Adam's nubby black Bible that she felt there, her memory groping for words of prayer and praise.

"Even, though I walk through the valley of the shadow of death, I will fear no evil," she started cautiously, "for you are with me; your rod and your staff, they comfort me. You. . . ." And then she trailed off. The word *anoint* was in there somewhere, but she couldn't remember what came next.

The coyotes howled again. New tears scalded her face.

"Oh, dearest God," she wept out loud. "I don't know how to pray anymore. I want to—oh, Jesus you know how much I want to!—but I can't remember how to start. I don't blame you for not wanting to listen. I don't blame you for not wanting to answer. But it's not *me* I'm really asking for . . . don't you see? It's Joey. He's your child too, and he's never done anything wrong. Please help me to find him. Please protect him. Please forgive me, Lord. Forgive me for so many things.''

It took Amy a moment to realize that she had, in spite of everything, managed to pray. Her face felt a little cooler, and a tiny rock wedged in the mud began to chafe one knee. Slowly she stood up, not expecting an answer to her awkward prayer but uplifted, somehow, by the knowledge that she'd made the attempt. Adam would have been proud of her.

A quick rush of tiny feet under a nearby tree caused her a moment's panic, but almost instantaneously she realized that the creature was too small to do her any harm. In a moment the silence was punctured again by three low hoots of an unseen owl. She wondered if the owl might be planning to devour the harmless creature in the bushes. It seemed odd to Amy that she'd never thought of owls as hunters because Orville the Owl was such a kindly soul. How nice it was to know that he and Irene had been granted permission to make a home up here near the summit after—

''That's it!'' Amy whispered in unabashed wonder as the image of a groundskeeper's cabin erected itself in her mind. ''That's it!'' she repeated, shouting the words out loud. ''Joey's at the cabin. He's safe with Orville and Irene! He walked up here until he found the cabin, got hungry and cold and went in! All I have to do is find it!''

Even in the darkness it was not too difficult for Amy to find the trail that led off from one side of Persistence Peak toward a tiny porch light in the distance. For the next forty minutes she never missed a step, never swerved in the wrong direction, never felt another moment's fear. Yet it was not until she reached the cabin and pounded on the door—to be instantly rewarded by the blessed sight of aging Irene the Queen with a small sleeping boy in her arms—that

Amy realized, quite abruptly, that not only had the Lord listened to her pathetic prayer: He had already answered it.

CHAPTER 13

THE SUN WAS SHINING so brightly in Amy's heart the next morning that she hardly noticed that a storm still raged outside. After a filling breakfast of pancakes and hot chocolate, Irene and Orville bundled their two charges into an ancient pickup and carted them down the hill to the main camp where Kay and Bill Shelby were waiting. While the pickup jumped and jostled down the dirt road from Persistence Peak, Amy had plenty of time to prepare herself for what lay ahead.

Long before Amy had reached the cabin, Orville had called Adam with news of his lost refugee. A second call, hours later, reported that Amy was also safe and sound but it seemed wiser to not to brave the rutted dirt road to the main camp in the dark. Amy had not asked to speak to Adam, who had spent hours combing the mountains in search of both of them. She did not want to think about what he would have said to her, even though she was certain she deserved every word. She was almost relieved that she'd already given up all hope of a future with this sterling man she loved; with luck, she could pretend that he couldn't hurt her anymore. It was enough that God had given Joey another chance. She would ask for nothing more.

Yet Amy couldn't help but be nervous as they drove into the camp. She *did* have to face all these people before she ran away. If Adam had taught her anything, it was how to stand up and face her problems. She had to thank Pillsie for staying at Timber Wolf overnight with her girls, and she had to say goodbye to Tiffany. Regardless of Trevor's expectations, she had forged a precious bond with the young girl and it would unforgivable to disappear without exchanging addresses and promises.

"Mom's really gonna be sorry she got the flu and missed this week at camp, huh, Amy?" Joey chirped brightly beside her, fully recovered from his night of fear. "What a story I'm gonna get to tell at school!"

Amy put her arm around him and hugged him freely. It had taken only a few tearful moments to put things right with this loving child of God. He would never doubt his sister's love for him again.

"Where's my mom and dad, Orville?" he asked the elderly man. "At the lodge?"

Orville shrugged and pushed his round glasses back up his nose. "I suspect breakfast is over, Joey. More than likely they're waiting for you at Grizzly, unless they've already crossed the Jordan."

A stab of trepidation pierced Amy's heart. "Crossed the Jordan?" she queried.

"Can't have the final morning's worship in the bowl when it's raining, Amy," he reminded her. "The service starts at ten, and it's five after right now. My best guess is that you'll find the whole passel of 'em up at the chapel." He looked at Amy with sudden insight. "Are you the one who's been leading the singing this week?"

She nodded.

"Thought so. Every night there's been the sweetest

sound drifting up to our place from the bowl. But last night—nothing. I thought maybe it was because of the rain."

From the other side of the truck Irene, who had been silent up till now, said quietly, "Orville, do you remember the last time Amy was here with her mother when she sang 'Amazing Grace'? I've never heard anything quite so heavenly."

New tension gripped Amy. She hadn't bargained on the chapel. Yes, she'd made her peace with the Lord. He'd come through for her and she was ready to serve Him for the rest of her life. But . . . "Amazing Grace" in the chapel? *Come on, Lord, isn't that asking a bit much for me this morning?*

Adam, of course, would have taken such a moment to retell the tale of Amos when God drafted him into his service. At first Amy was relieved that he wasn't there to remind her. But then she realized, with a sharp, heart-numbing clarity, that it no longer really mattered whether Adam was there or not when it came to faith. Her faith. He had taught her everything she needed to know this week: *Trust in the Lord.* She had and she would, and she would forever be grateful to Adam Reed for having the strength and courage to have shown her the road back.

As they rumbled into the circle of pines that had greeted her only six short days ago, Amy remembered a promise that she had made to Adam that first night in his study . . . a promise to let him know if she ever found her way back to Jesus. Somehow she'd have to tell him what had happened to her last night . . . and that meant she'd have to see him alone.

Amy climbed out of the dripping pickup and looked up the mountain at the rustic cross that hung over the chapel. She shook her head, then took Joey's hand and started up the trail with only a quick hug and thank you for Irene and Orville. She didn't even hesitate as she led her brother across the tiny bridge above the stream.

The two of them slipped into the back of the church just as Adam began to preach. The little sanctuary was so crowded that he did not notice, or pretended not to notice, the nature of the commotion in the back corner. He didn't miss a beat as bit Bill Shelby—red-faced and deeply moved—stood up, trembling, to take his daughter in his arms. Nor did he hesitate when Kay Shelby clung to her small boy with fresh tears, then took Amy into her arms as her new daughter whispered, "I love him, Kay. I love you. I'm so sorry. I was so wrong. Everything is different now."

But when Amy freed herself from her family and stood, perfectly still, to study and memorize her beloved Adam's face, his voice died in a sudden hushed and choking sound. A thousand hurts and broken hopes swept across his features as she stood there: his week of agony and self-denial, his fervent prayers and ardent hope for her redemption; his anguish and self-reproach for the way he had been forced to hurt her. And then, very slowly, something new washed over his face.

Joy. The light in her eyes shone so brightly it obliterated his own darkness, and it was clear that he knew that every moment of his personal torture had been worth this end. She had found her way Home! It didn't matter how. It didn't matter whether it was because of Adam or because of someone else, or because of some burst of growing in Amy herself. What mattered was that she was whole again . . . she belonged to Him again! She had crossed the Jordan.

Have you ever given much thought to the demands of being a pastor's wife? Linda didn't want to spend every Thanksgiving with some lonesome stranger at the family table . . . to pray at the ladies' luncheons and take over the preaching when I had laryngitis. . . .

The words chased through Amy's mind as she

watched this intensely Christian man she loved. He was in the middle of a sermon, yet so blinded by great Light that he was, for the moment, simply unable to speak. He would be sorry later, she was sure; embarrassed that he'd revealed himself so utterly to all these people. And it was her fault.

Without an instant's hesitation, Amy leaned down to Kay and whispered words she could never have imagined she'd be able to say. "I want you to play for me. I've got to sing 'Amazing Grace.'"

To say that Kay looked stunned would be an understatement. She studied her hands as though she wanted to be sure she had all ten fingers; but she looked around the room for the ancient piano and headed toward it, hymnal in hand, while Amy marched up to the knotty pine pulpit and gently edged Adam aside. By the time she sang the first note, Kay was ready.

It was Bill Shelby who was not prepared. His eyes, suddenly moist and red, went from his wife to his daughter and back again before he covered face and slumped onto the nearest redwood stump, shaking his head in joyous disbelief as he witnessed his daughter's full redemption.

Through many dangers, toils, and snares
I have already come!
'Tis grace hath brought me safe thus far,
And grace will lead me home.

Amy's beautiful voice filled the room and defeated the rain. Tiny campers felt the Grace, some for the very first time. Every note that Kay Shelby played on the battered, sacred piano sealed her new bonding with her once-resistant daughter; every trembling word shouted Adam Reed's astounding realization that the woman he loved was now a person who would always walk hand in hand with the Lord.

In the back of the room, Tiffany Grant wrapped her tiny fingers around her father's warm, quiet hand, and little Joey Shelby threw both arms around his weeping father.

"It's okay, Daddy," he crooned with all the sweetness his young heart could offer. "Everything's going to be all right now. Amy told me so. And God's the one who told Amy. . . ."

In Amy's mind the next few hours lasted for days. It seemed that every single person in the camp had to hear the entire story of her night on the mountain and Joey's night with Orville and Irene. Amy, on the other hand, had to listen to Trevor's version of their hike down the trail, and then Tiffany's version, which was considerably less eventful and probably more accurate. But when they were alone, Tiffany, eyes shining, reported, "Those kids would have gotten lost on that trail without me, Amos. Daddy really didn't know where to go and his foot hurt him a lot. He needed me, Amos. He really did."

Amy shared her joy with a quick hug. Trevor had already made it clear that Camp Colina had worked the family miracle he'd prayed for. Not only had Tiffany led Amy's mini-choir in singing "Let Us Break Bread Together on Our Knees" the night before, but she'd also insisted that Trevor take Holy Communion with her. "'Cause Amos would want us to." The greatest surprise in Amy's week was that she was sorry that she'd missed the opportunity to take Communion herself.

"Just keep talking to him, Tiffy," she reminded her young friend. "Don't shut him out. Even when he's wrong. Tell him he's wrong, but don't stop talking to him."

Tiffany nodded. "He says he wants me to live with him for the rest of the summer and then I can go back to my grandma's if I want to." She looked perplexed. "My grandma's gonna miss me."

Amy gave her a reassuring smile. "I'll be praying for you, honey, now that I remember how."

202

Tiffany grinned. "I might even learn how, too. Daddy says we're going to start going to church, just the two of us. Summit knows some preacher guy at a church near Daddy's house. . . ." She hesitated. "Do you think he'll be like Summit?"

Amy struggled with her feelings. There was no way to express the sense of joy and pain, victory and loss, that would always accompany her thoughts of Adam. The only thing she was sure of was that she would never forget him. He might, from time to time, remember Amy. But when he did she suspected that it would only be because she represented a tormented soul he'd restored to the Lord . . . and visible proof that he'd triumphed over his own mortal weakness.

"Well, sweetheart," Amy said out loud to Tiffany, "You know there's nobody *just* like Adam, but I'd guess that any friend of his would be a good person to know."

Tiffany nodded with a bit more confidence. "Do you think the church will have Sunday school? With other kids?"

This time they shared the grin, knowing how far they'd both come together. "I'm sure of it, Tiffy." She considered adding a word of encouragement to attend, but decided against it.

Reading her mind, Tiffany declared, "I'll make you a deal, Amos. If you'll promise to teach Sunday school when you go home, I'll promise to go to church with Daddy. Then I can pretend that we're really there together."

Unspeakably moved, Amy pulled the young girl close for a farewell hug. "It's a deal, Tiffany. The Lord will always tie us together."

A whistle brought Amy's attention to the pine log parking lot. Trevor waved goodbye to Amy, not for the first time, and beckoned for Tiffany to join him. She gave Amy a quick, embarrassed kiss on the cheek before she bounded off toward her father. "I'll write to you, Amos!" she promised, then grinned up at Trevor as he ruffled her hair. They climbed into the car together and drove off in a flurry of loving farewells.

A few minutes later Julie Ann came up to hug Amy goodbye, her eyes damp with tears. "You're the best counselor I ever had, Amos," she whispered, her little voice so sweet and sincere that Amy almost forgot that she was the *only* counselor that Julie Ann had ever had.

The rest of the farewells weren't nearly as poignant for Amy, but that was only because she had yet to say goodbye to Adam. She knew that once she saw his face for the last time, she would be in no condition to speak to anyone.

"We've got two cars here, Amy," her father pointed out as he finished loading up the children's bags. He was still embarrassed at the way he'd fallen apart in the chapel, but Amy knew that the next time they were alone the very last traces of pain between them would be swept away. "Do you want one of us to ride with you for company or do you have other plans? There's room for Cindy and Nathan with us."

A great sadness suddenly filled Amy. She didn't want to be alone today; she wanted to be with someone who knew what it was like to ache for a man who didn't want you, who knew you needed to cry and didn't expect you to explain yourself. Someone like a mother.

"I'll ride with Amy," Kay announced unexpectedly. "I've got some ideas for Sunday anthems I want to go over with her."

Amy turned to Kay in astonishment. Her stepmother's brown eyes were quiet but warm. She knew! How had she realized, in the briefest of contacts, that Amy was in love with Adam?

She offered Amy a kind, cautious smile and whispered, "You go tell him goodbye. I'll be here if you want to talk about it."

Amy gave her a tearful hug, wondering how on earth she had resisted this woman's loving acceptance for so long! Yet suddenly she knew that she would need privacy in her first few minutes apart from Adam. Directly to Kay she whispered, "You go on ahead. I need to be alone for a while. But I promise to talk to you later."

She hugged Kay and her father, then clenched Joey for a long, wordless moment as he kissed her goodbye. He broke loose, singing boisterously, and followed Cindy and Nathan into the car as Amy slowly approached the meadow. She knew she could not avoid her last farewell any longer.

Finding Adam was not difficult. Finding a moment's privacy with him was impossible.

He looked like he had the first day of camp— surrounded by tiny campers, piles of luggage and enthusiastic camp counselors. He wore clean but faded blue jeans and a yellow sweatshirt printed with an unadorned symbol of a fish. He didn't seem to notice that it had started raining again.

"I love this man," Amy whispered to herself. "I must accept that, and try to live with it. It changes nothing." But the great aching throb inside her refused to believe it.

Suddenly she knew she couldn't face him amidst a crush of children and superficial farewells. The look on his face when he'd heard her first morning notes of "Amazing Grace" had reassured her that she was, as he had once told her, very special to him. Not in the same way that *he* was special to *her*, of course, but special enough to appreciate her need for a private goodbye.

Only after she had waved goodbye to her family and headed toward the bowl did Amy realize that she wasn't really quite ready to leave Camp Colina. She wasn't ready to leave the pines, the blue jays, the yellow jackets during meals. All week she'd fenced with her feelings in the chapel, at the bowl, at morning watch. Day by day she'd grown a little stronger . . . and a little closer to the Lord. But now that she and Jesus were finally reunited, she wanted a little more time to visit with Him! A few more days or hours to luxuriate in the joyous spiritual home of her youth . . . and the precious memories of her mother that were no longer laced with such bittersweet pain. Yet Amy knew that just as Adam had once been the reason she'd stayed at Camp Colina, he was now the reason she would have to leave. His presence guaranteed her a whole new collection of painful memories. She was ready to seek the Lord elsewhere.

Dear Lord, help me to face Adam with courage and gratitude, she prayed in the silence of the bowl. *Help me to leave him feeling only joy for what he's done for me. Don't let me saddle him with any more of my pain.*

With a final farewell glance at the spot by the fire where Adam had made it so irrevocably clear that he could never love her as a woman, Amy tugged on the hood of her sweat shirt and headed back toward the sign that had welcomed her to Camp Colina.

The meadow was nearly empty now, so Amy headed straight for Adam. She waited until he poked his head out of a car full of kids and plunged toward another one. She was certain that this last sight of his dimpled smile would haunt her always.

"Excuse me, Adam," she interrupted him formally. "It looks like almost everybody's gone now, so—"

He cast her a look of surprise . . . or perhaps irritation. "Can't it wait till I finish up here, Amy? I won't be more than a few minutes."

Stung, she tossed back, "I didn't realize I had to stand in line just to say goodbye. Nobody else here had to!"

"Just to—" His eyes narrowed, fully focused on her now. His lips seemed tight. "Are you . . . *leaving,*

Amy?'' He sounded stunned. Even if the tone of his voice had not arrested her, the disbelief on his face would have. It seemed incredible to him that she would even consider going anywhere!

Dear God, is it possible that he has changed his mind? It is possible. . . . Amy struggled to restrain the desperate new hope within her. ''Is there . . . ,'' she swallowed the words, '' . . . some reason . . . why . . . I should stay?''

Fresh pain whipped his features, and the rain seemed to intensify his longing. His eyes were haunted. ''Amy . . . I . . . rather thought that after . . . last night . . . we might have some things to say to each other.''

He waited a lifetime for her response. Amy wanted to throw her arms around him and spill out exactly what she longed to tell him and exactly what she longed to hear. She wanted to whisper that she loved him in a way that would never change, in a way that went far beyond her gratitude for all he had done for her. She wanted to hear him declare that now that she belonged to the Lord it would no longer be wrong for her to belong to Adam Reed. She longed to kiss him, just this once, to savor the memory for the rest of her life. But the look in his eyes stopped her. All the hunger, the anguish, the uncertainty that she'd read there before still lingered, and suddenly she was sure that nothing had changed.

''I . . . think you've already made your position pretty clear, Adam.'' She forced out the words. ''I think it would only be . . . more difficult for both of us to drag it out. I just wanted to . . . thank you for reuniting me with the Lord. I left your . . . Bible and things . . . in your study.''

''*No*.'' It was a slow, anguished word that matched the pain in his eyes. ''You've got to keep the Bible. At least that—''

''I've got one of my own at home, Adam, and I'm

207

not afraid to read it now. You did your job. You were true to your beliefs. You don't have to worry about me anymore.''

''Amy....'' The word seemed to strangle him. ''Please don't leave like this. I thought . . . I wanted to say goodbye to all these people so we could be alone. We're always being interrupted . . . and this time it's important that....'' He broke off uncertainly. ''Please don't leave me,'' he finished on a ragged breath. ''Please don't leave me like this.''

Before she could answer, another carload came by. It was all Amy could do to wave goodbye to Grand Slam and Pinky. Her pulse was galloping with wild, impractical anticipation. Adam's anguish had somehow filled her with delirious new hope. Nothing in his face or voice conveyed the sense of a man who wanted to say goodbye!

The next car stopped to let out four small children, all of whom swarmed around Adam for a farewell hug. Two more cars ambled by in quick succession, but he didn't need to worry about Amy disappearing while he said goodbye to the campers. She was not about to move the width of a blade of grass until he told her to go.

Ten minutes—or maybe ten hours—passed before the two of them finally stood alone in the meadow. They were both dripping wet and acutely aware that only one car remained in the pine pole lot—a dusty white Maverick, nose pointed down the hill, ready to crawl away from Camp Colina forever. A lone woodpecker worked on the side of Grizzly Cabin while Amy waited for Adam to speak. Two squirrels played tag in front of the lodge.

Slowly he turned to face her, his eyes a turbulent sea shade that left her longing to give him everything he had ever wanted from her even though she was still afraid that he'd decided not to ask.

''We ought to get out of the rain,'' Amy whispered,

208

quivering inside. It wasn't a particularly brilliant opening line, but she couldn't think of anything else to say. If he didn't want her forever, she needed to know it this instant. She needed to accept it and get on with her life. If by some miracle he had something more hopeful to tell her, she desperately needed to hear it right now . . . before she dissolved while waiting for her deliverance.

"Amy. . . ," he breathed, just inches from her face. "Were you . . . really going to leave? You really didn't know. . . ." His voice trailed off as he swallowed deeply. His face took on the Light she'd seen in the chapel, then changed into a mask of confusion. "Have you changed your mind? Or is it . . . asking too much of you to . . . forgive me for hurting you? Do you really believe I thought you were . . . somehow . . . not good enough for me?"

Suddenly she knew this was not a time for fear or hesitation. Adam's eyes called out his love for her and mirrored her own uncertainty. All week she had tried to hide her feelings from this man, and yet now, Amy realized, if she didn't have the courage to risk revealing them, she could lose him forever.

"I love you, Adam Reed," she whispered against the rain. "That's not ever going to change."

At first he did not answer. His eyes darkened with a host of feelings she could not read. He brushed his wet hair out of his face and moved close enough to touch her.

Then he *did* touch her, but not like any man had ever touched her before. In a slow, pristine gesture of unmistakable Scriptural intent, Adam lifted his thumb to stroke one of his own ribs, and then placed his whole hand over one of Amy's. She felt the warmth of his fingertips against her waist as he quoted simply, " 'This is now the bone of my bone and flesh of my flesh. She shall be called woman because she was taken out of man.' "

Only two short days ago Amy had read those very words at Adam's urging, so she had no difficulty remembering what came next. In a hushed whisper she continued, " 'For this cause a man shall leave his father and his mother, and shall cleave to his wife; and they shall become. . . .' " She gasped as she realized the magical word of life-time love she had just quoted. She could not go on! Not with his eyes, his beautiful, soul-shattering blue eyes, asking, pleading, *begging* her to share his life with him!

"*Adam?*" she breathed in joyful disbelief.

He could have answered her question with paragraphs of reassurance, but he wasted no more time on words. With all the sweet yearning she had even imagined he felt for her, he wrapped both arms around Amy's shoulders and claimed her rain-washed lips with his own. It was a kiss that offered her everything, denied her nothing, promised her a lifetime of loving and faith.

In that instant Amy knew that there would never come a time when her life did not revolve around this man whose love had just merged with her own. The Lord had sent her to the mountains for many reasons, and He had carried out his plan. Adam had given her the Lord, and the Lord had given her Adam. She had never felt more blessed. She was surrounded by love, surrounded by family, and surrounded by Adam's strong and passionate arms.

Despite the eagerness of Amy's response, there came a time when Adam released her ever so slightly, pulling back enough to watch her eyes, enough to hear her answer to his Biblical proposal. But she had no words to give him; love and joy trampled her faculty of speech. She knew that her longing to share her life with him was painted on her face like a rainbow; yet still he wanted more. Overwhelmed and unsteady, Amy gripped Adam's waist.

It was the only reply he needed, but she kissed him again just the same.

ABOUT THE AUTHOR

SUZANNE PIERSON ELLISON comes from a long line of ministers and has been known to preach, herself, on occasion! She writes, however, from a deep need to bring about reconciliation in those who are estranged from family members or from God. Mrs. Ellison is a bilingual teacher in southern California.

A Letter To Our Readers

Dear Reader:

Pioneering is an exhilarating experience, filled with opportunities for exploring new frontiers. The Zondervan Corporation is proud to be the first major publisher to launch a series of inspirational romances designed to inspire and uplift as well as to provide wholesome entertainment. In order that we might better contribute to your reading enjoyment, we would appreciate your taking a few minutes to respond to the following questions and return to:

> Anne Severance, Editor
> The Zondervan Publishing House
> 1415 Lake Drive, S.E.
> Grand Rapids, Michigan   49506

1. Did you enjoy reading ONE MORE RIVER?

   ☐ Very much. I would like to see more books by this author!
   ☐ Moderately
   ☐ I would have enjoyed it more if _____

2. Where did you purchase this book? _____

3. What influenced your decision to purchase this book?

   ☐ Cover   ☐ Back cover copy
   ☐ Title   ☐ Friends
   ☐ Publicity   ☐ Other _____

4. Please rate the following elements from 1 (poor) to 10 (superior).

☐ Heroine   ☐ Plot
☐ Hero   ☐ Inspirational theme
☐ Setting   ☐ Secondary characters

5. Which settings would you like to see in future Serenade/Saga Books?

_____ _____

_____ _____

6. What are some inspirational themes you would like to see treated in future books?

_____ _____

_____ _____

7. Would you be interested in reading other Serenade/Serenata or Serenade/Saga Books?

☐ Very interested
☐ Moderately interested
☐ Not interested

8. Please indicate your age range:

☐ Under 18   ☐ 25–34   ☐ 46–55
☐ 18–24   ☐ 35–45   ☐ Over 55

9. Would you be interested in a Serenade book club? If so, please give us your name and address:

Name _____

Occupation _____

Address _____

City _____ State _____ Zip _____

Serenade Serenata Books are inspirational romances in contemporary settings, designed to bring you a joyful, heart-lifting reading experience.

Serenade Serenata books available in your local bookstore:

    Watch for other books in the *Serenade Serenata* (contemporary) series coming soon:

Serenade Saga Books are inspirational romances in historical settings, designed to bring you a joyful, heart-lifting reading experience.

Serenade Saga books available in your local bookstore:

#1 SUMMER SNOW, Sandy Dengler
#2 CALL HER BLESSED, Jeanette Gilge
#3 INA, Karen Baker Kletzing
#4 JULIANA OF CLOVER HILL,
     Brenda Knight Graham
#5 SONG OF THE NEREIDS, Sandy Dengler
#6 ANNA'S ROCKING CHAIR,
     Elaine Watson
#7 IN LOVE'S OWN TIME,
     Susan C. Feldhake
#8 YANKEE BRIDE, Jane Peart
#9 LIGHT OF MY HEART, Kathleen Karr
#10 LOVE BEYOND SURRENDER,
     Susan C. Feldhake
#11 ALL THE DAYS AFTER SUNDAY,
     Jeanette Gilge
#12 WINTERSPRING, Sandy Dengler
#13 HAND ME DOWN THE DAWN,
     Mary Harwell Sayler
#14 REBEL BRIDE, Jane Peart
#15 SPEAK SOFTLY, LOVE, Kathleen Yapp
#16 FROM THIS DAY FORWARD, Kathleen Karr
#17 THE RIVER BETWEEN, Jacquelyn Cook
#18 VALIANT BRIDE, Jane Peart
#19 WAIT FOR THE SUN, Maryn Langer

Watch for other books in the *Serenade Saga* series coming soon:

#20 KINCAID OF CRIPPLE CREEK, Peggy Darty
#21 LOVE'S GENTLE JOURNEY, Kay Cornelius